THE EMOTION COLLECTOR

RAVEN FONTAINE

Indie Pen Press

TURNING DREAMS INTO BESTSELLERS

Indie Pen Press
600 1st Ave Ste 330 PMB 582144
Seattle, Washington 98104-2246
IndiePenPress.com

First Edition: September 2024

The characters and events portrayed in this book are fictitious. Any similarity to real persons, living or dead, is coincidental and not intended by the author.

Paperback ISBN 979-8-9919463-3-9

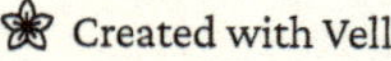 Created with Vellum

PROLOGUE: THE GREAT PACIFICATION

Dr. Elena Thorne's fingers trembled as she adjusted the microphone. The weight of billions of lives pressed down on her shoulders, making every breath a struggle. She scanned the sea of anxious faces, their fear palpable in the stuffy auditorium air.

"Ladies and gentlemen of the World Health Organization," she began, her voice steadier than she felt, "we stand on the precipice of human extinction."

A murmur went through the crowd. Elena's gaze fell on a man in the front row, his face etched with worry lines. She recognized him as Dr. Yamamoto, her mentor.

"Elena," he said, his voice breaking, "there must be another way. The empathy pandemic -"

"Is spreading faster than any virus in history," Elena interrupted. She tapped her tablet, and holographic images came to life behind her—cities in chaos. Hospitals are overflowing—stock markets are in free fall.

"Three billion infected in the last month alone," she continued. "The human brain was not meant to feel the pain of the entire world. We are collapsing under the weight of our own emotions."

A woman stood up, her eyes red. "My daughter..." she choked out. "She hasn't stopped crying in weeks. She feels everything, Dr. Thorne. Everything!"

Elena's heart tightened. How often had she heard similar stories? How many sleepless nights had she spent trying to find a solution?

"I know," she said. "And that is why we are here today." She took a deep breath. "Ladies and gentlemen, I present to you The Emotional Regulation Initiative."

The hologram shifted, showing complex neural pathways and chemical formulas. Elena began her explanation, her words precise and measured.

"By targeting specific areas of the brain, we can suppress the neural circuits responsible for emotional processing. We retain our intelligence and our ability to reason and create. But the chaos of uncontrolled emotion? We can leave that behind."

The room erupted in a cacophony of voices.

"You're talking about lobotomizing the entire human race!" someone shouted.

"It's not a lobotomy," Elena countered, her voice rising. "It's salvation. A world without war, without heartbreak, without..."

"Without what makes us human!" Dr. Yamamoto interjected, now standing. "Elena, listen to yourself. This isn't the answer."

Elena's fingers clenched into fists. She could feel it building inside her, this tidal wave of emotions that threatened to drown her, just like everyone else.

"Then what is it?" she demanded, her composure breaking. "Do you have a better solution? Because I've watched people tear themselves apart, crushed under the weight of global suffering. I've held my own daughter as she cried out in sympathetic agony for people she'd never met!"

The room fell silent. Elena found herself breathing hard, tears stinging her eyes. She blinked them back and forced her voice to calm.

"We have the power to end suffering," she said, more quietly now. "To create a world of peace and progress. Yes, there is a cost. But the alternative is extinction."

Hours later, Elena stood at her office window, watching the city below. Sirens wailed in the distance. Another riot? Another mass suicide? She closed her eyes, trying to block it all out.

A soft knock on the door made her turn. "Come in."

Dr. Yamamoto entered, his face grave. "The WHO has made its decision," he said.

Elena's heart raced. "And?"

He sighed. "They have approved the initiative. Global implementation will begin next week.

Relief and fear warred inside her. She'd won. Then why did victory taste so bitter?

"Elena," Yamamoto said, "I hope you know what you're doing."

She turned back to the window, unable to meet his gaze. "So do I," she whispered.

As Yamamoto's footsteps faded, Elena reached into her desk drawer and pulled out a photograph. A baby girl stared back at her, tiny fists raised as if in defiance, eyes a swirl of emotion not yet understood.

"I'm sorry, Aria," Elena murmured, tracing her daughter's face. "I hope one day you'll understand. This is the only way I know how to save you."

She put the photo down and turned to her computer. Taking a deep breath, she began to type:

Project Rebirth: Phase 1 approved. Emotional suppression protocols completed. Implementation is to commence as planned.

Her finger hovered over the send button. For a moment, just a moment, doubt crept in. "We are creating a world without pain," she muttered. "But at what cost?"

The doubt passed. She sent the report.

Outside her window, the sun set on a world on the brink of transformation. A world about to trade its tears and laughter, its anger and joy, for the promise of peace.

A world about to be changed forever.

ONE
THE COLLECTOR

Twenty-five years had passed since Dr. Elena Thorne introduced the Emotional Regulation Initiative, reshaping society into a world of logic and order. The little girl in the photograph, the one Elena had tried to protect, had grown into a young woman. Aria Thorne, now twenty-three, bore little resemblance to the emotional infant her mother had once cradled. Raised in the new world order, Aria had become the very thing her mother had both feared and created: an emotion collector tasked with maintaining the delicate balance of a society free from the chaos of emotion.

Aria's footsteps echoed through the sterile corridors of the Emotion Regulation Center. The harsh fluorescent lights overhead cast no shadows, leaving no place for secrets to hide. Just the way the Global Harmony Council liked it.

She adjusted her gray uniform, her fingers brushing the silver insignia that marked her as an Emotion Collector. The familiar weight should have been comforting, but today, it felt like a shackle.

As she approached the briefing room, a flicker of... something... went through her. Aria paused, frowning. Not a feeling - those had been purged from her long ago. No, it was more like an echo—a ghost of a feeling.

"You're late, Collector Thorne."

The voice brought Aria back to the present. Her superior, Director Kaine, stood in the doorway, his face a mask of calm disapproval.

"My apologies, Director," Aria said, her own voice calm and unemotional. "It won't happen again."

Kaine nodded, stepping aside to let her enter. "Make sure it doesn't. Lateness is inefficient."

The briefing room was small and austere, like everything else in this world. A handful of other Collectors sat around a round table, their faces as blank as clean wiped slates. Aria took a seat, ignoring the hollow feeling in her chest.

"Now that we're all here," Kaine began, his gaze lingering on Aria for a moment, "let's review today's assignments."

In the center of the table, a holographic display flickered to life, showing a map of the city. Red dots pulsed at various points, each representing a potential emotional disturbance.

"We have detected an increase in residual emotions in Sector 7," Kaine continued. "Collector Chen, you'll take the northwest quadrant. Collector Thorne, you'll take the southeast."

Aria nodded and studied the map. Sector 7 - the old art district. Even after twenty-five years, she still clung to the remnants of her emotional past.

"What's the nature of the disturbance?" asked Chen, his voice as flat as if he were asking about the weather.

Kaine tapped the screen, zooming in on one of the red dots. "Mostly low-level nostalgia and melancholy. Nothing too serious, but we can't risk it spreading."

"Understood," Aria said. "Standard extraction protocols?"

"Affirmative," Kaine replied. "Remember, your job is to collect and contain. Do not deal with the emotion itself."

As if she needed reminding. Aria had been doing this job for five years. She knew the risks of emotional contamination better than anyone.

The briefing ended, and the Collectors filed out of the room. As Aria turned to leave, Kaine's voice stopped her.

"One moment, Collector Thorne."

Aria turned and met his gaze. "Yes, Director?"

Kaine studied her for a long moment, his eyes searching for... what? Aria kept her face carefully neutral.

"Your extraction numbers have been... inconsistent lately," he said. "Is there a problem I should be aware of?"

Aria's heart rate increased slightly - a typical physiological reaction. "No problem, Director. I've just been dealing with more complex cases. I assure you, my efficiency remains optimal."

Kaine nodded. "See that it stays that way. You're one of our finest collectors, Aria. It would be... unfortunate if that changed."

"Understood, sir." Aria turned to leave, then paused. Have there been any updates on the research into emotionally resistant individuals?

A flicker of something - surprise? Suspicion? - crossed Kaine's face before it settled back into impassivity. "This information is classified, Collector Thorne. Concentrate on your assigned duties."

"Of course. My apologies."

As Aria left the Emotional Regulation Center, she couldn't shake the feeling that something was... wrong. But that was impossible. Feelings were the enemy. Feelings were chaos.

The streets of Sector 7 were as orderly as any other part of the city, but there was a different energy here. The buildings, once vibrant with color and life, were now gray and uniform. But if you looked closely, you could still see traces of the murals beneath the paint, ghosts of a more passionate past.

Aria's wrist device beeped, alerting her to nearby emotional activity. She followed the signal to a small cafe, its windows dark and dusty.

Inside, an older man sat alone at a table, staring at an old photograph. As Aria approached, she could see the slight trembling in his hands, the shine in his eyes that didn't entirely turn to tears.

"Sir," she said in a calm voice, "I need you to come with me."

The man looked up, his eyes scanning Aria's face. "I... I don't understand. I just had a cup of tea."

Aria looked at the table. There was no cup or saucer—just the photo and the man's shaking hands.

"Sir, you're having an emotional episode. I'm here to help."

The man's brow furrowed. "Episode? No, I... I just remembered. My wife, you know. Today would have been our anniversary."

A pang of... something... echoed through Aria's chest. She pushed it aside and focused on the task at hand.

"I understand," she said, though of course she didn't. Couldn't. "But remembering like this, it's not healthy. It's not efficient. Let me help you."

Aria reached out, her fingers almost touching the man's wrinkled hand. With a touch, she could absorb the emotion and leave it alone, empty.

But the man drew back, clutching the photograph to his chest. "No," he said, his voice suddenly stronger. "No, I don't want to forget. Even if it hurts, I don't want to forget."

Aria hesitated. Protocol dictated that she call for backup and have the man forcibly treated, but something stopped her—that echo again, that ghost of a feeling she couldn't name.

"Sir," she said, her voice low, "I can't leave you like this. It's my job to collect these emotions, to keep our society stable."

The man looked at her, really looked at her, and for a moment, Aria felt exposed. It was as if this frail, emotional old man could see through her well-constructed facade.

"Is this really what you want?" he asked. "A stable society where no one remembers? Where no one feels?"

Aria opened her mouth to answer, to recite the mantras she'd been taught since childhood. Emotions are chaos. Logic is peace. But the words wouldn't come.

Instead, she found herself saying, "Five minutes. I'll give you five minutes, and then you must come with me."

The man nodded, a small smile touching his lips. "Thank you," he whispered, turning back to his photo.

As Aria watched him, that hollow feeling in her chest grew. And for the first time in her life, she wondered if he was trying to tell her something.

Five minutes. Five minutes that would break every rule she'd ever known.

Five minutes that would change everything.

TWO
ECHOES OF FEELING

Aria's wrist device chirped, breaking the silence. Five minutes were up.

"Sir," she said, her voice softer than the protocol required, "it's time."

The old man looked up from his photograph, eyes glistening with unshed tears. "Just... just one more moment."

Aria's throat tightened. A physiological reaction, she told herself. Nothing more. "I can't. Please, don't make this difficult."

The man nodded and stood with a sigh that seemed to carry the weight of years. His fingers trembled as he slipped the photograph into his pocket. Aria pretended not to notice.

As they walked out of the café, Aria felt the stares of the passersby. Their faces were blank, but their eyes followed her and the older man with an intensity that made her skin crawl. She quickened her pace.

The extraction center loomed ahead, a sleek monolith of glass and steel. As they approached, Aria felt the older man stiffen beside her.

"What will happen to me?" he asked, his voice barely above a whisper.

Aria swallowed hard. "You will be... helped. The disturbing emotions will be removed, and you'll be able to return to your normal routine."

"And my memories?"

She hesitated. "They will still be there. Just... without the emotional attachment."

The man stopped walking, forcing Aria to turn and face him. "Then what's the point?" he asked, his voice suddenly sharp. "What's the point of remembering if I can't feel it?"

For a moment, Aria was at a loss. She'd never thought about that question before. She never allowed herself to. "It's... it's for the greater good," she said, sounding hollow even to her own ears. "For societal stability."

The man's eyes searched her face as if looking for something Aria herself didn't know was there. "Is that what you really believe?"

Before she could answer, a voice cut through the air. "Collector Thorne."

Aria turned to see Director Kaine approaching, his face a mask of calm efficiency. "Sir, I was just bringing-"

"I can see that," Kaine interrupted. His eyes darted to the older man, then back to Aria. "You're late with your report. I trust there were no... complications?"

Aria straightened, forcing her face into neutral lines. "No, sir. Just a routine extraction."

Kaine's eyebrow arched slightly. "Routine extractions don't usually take this long, Collector Thorne."

"I..." Aria's mind raced. "The subject required additional time to comply. I thought it more efficient to wait rather than call for backup."

"I see." Kaine's gaze bored into her, and Aria fought the urge to fidget. "Well, let's not waste any more time. I'll take it from here."

Before Aria could protest, Kaine grabbed the older man by the arm and led him toward the extraction center. The mance, his eyes meeting Aria's. She saw something in them she'd never seen before: glanced back on a mixture of fear and... was it pity?

As the doors closed behind them, Aria let out a breath she hadn't realized she was holding. Her hands were shaking. She clenched them into fists, wishing they would stop.

"Collector Thorne?"

Aria jumped, spinning around to face the new voice. It belonged to Maya, another Collector she'd trained with years ago. Maya's face was as impassive as ever, but her brow had a slight furrow.

"Are you... functioning optimally?" Maya asked the closest thing to concern their emotionless society allowed.

Aria forced a nod. "Yes, of course. Just... finishing up a complex extraction."

Maya tilted her head slightly. "I see. Well, we've been assigned to patrol Sector 9 together. Shall we proceed?"

"Right. Yes." Aria fell in step beside Maya, grateful for the distraction.

As they walked, a public service announcement blared from nearby loudspeakers: "Emotion is chaos. Order is peace. Report any signs of emotional aberration to your nearest collector."

Aria had heard that message a thousand times before, but today, it was getting on her nerves. She looked at Maya and wondered if her colleague felt the same way. But Maya's face was completely blank, her eyes staring straight ahead.

They turned a corner and entered Sector 9. Once the city's entertainment district, it now housed rows of identical apartment blocks and efficiency centers. But if you looked closely, you could still see faded posters peeking out from under layers of regulation gray paint.

"Maya," Aria found herself saying, "do you ever wonder about... before?"

Maya's steps faltered for a split second. "Before what?"

"Before the Emotional Regulation Initiative. What it was like when people... felt things."

For a long moment, Maya was silent. When she finally spoke, her voice was low. "This kind of speculation is not productive, Collector Thorne. Or safe."

Aria nodded, chastened. "Of course not. You're right. I don't know what I was thinking."

They continued their patrol in silence, but Aria's mind was anything but quiet. The older man's words echoed in her mind: "What's the point of remembering if I can't feel it?"

As they passed an abandoned theater, Aria's wrist device beeped. She frowned and tapped the screen. "This is weird. I'm picking up an emotional signature, but it's... inconsistent."

Maya looked at the device. "Could it be a malfunction? We should report it and request a diagnostic."

But Aria was already moving toward the theater's boarded-up entrance. "It'll be quicker if we check it out ourselves. Come on."

With a barely audible sigh, Maya followed.

The theater's interior was dark and musty, years of neglect evident in every corner. Aria's device led them to the stage, its screen pulsing with increasing intensity.

"There's someone here," Aria whispered, though she wasn't sure why she felt the need to lower her voice.

As if in response, a figure stepped out from behind a tattered curtain. A tall and lean man with tousled copper hair and eyes that seemed to glow in the dim light.

"Well," he said, a crooked smile playing on his lips, "I wasn't expecting company."

Aria's breath caught in her throat. There was something about him, something she couldn't quite put her finger on. Her device was going haywire, readings spiking and dropping erratically.

"Sir," Maya said, her voice calm, "you are in a restricted area. We're going to have to take you in for emotional evaluation and extraction."

The man's smile widened, and Aria felt an unfamiliar warmth in her chest. "I'm afraid that won't be possible," he said, his eyes locked with Aria's. "You see, I have no emotions for you to extract."

Aria's mind reeled. It wasn't possible. Everyone had emotions, buried deep or otherwise. Everyone except...

"You're emotion-resistant," she breathed.

The man winked. "Got it in one. Now the question is... what are you going to do about it?"

As Aria stared at him, torn between duty and curiosity she'd never felt before, she realized that her world was about to change far more than she could have ever imagined.

THREE
SHADES OF GRAY

Aria's heart pounded in her chest, a physiological response she couldn't control. The emotion-resistant man stood before her, his crooked smile unwavering. Behind her, she could feel Maya tensing, ready to call for backup.

"Maya," Aria said, her voice low and steady despite the turmoil inside her, "give us a moment."

Maya's eyebrows rose a fraction - the closest thing to surprise in her emotionless world. "Protocol dictates-"

"I know what protocol dictates," Aria cut her off, perhaps too sharply. She softened her tone. "Trust me. Please."

For a long moment, Maya said nothing. Then, with a slight nod, she stepped back. "Two minutes, Collector Thorne. Then I'll call it in."

Aria turned back to the man, whose smile had grown into something almost... mischievous? Was that the right word? It had been so long since she'd seen real expressions, she wasn't sure she could trust her interpretations anymore.

"You have a name?" she asked, trying to keep her voice professional.

The man's eyes twinkled. Twinkled, actually. Aria hadn't known eyes could do that outside of old stories. "Evan," he said. "And you are Aria Thorne. Daughter of the great Dr. Elena Thorne, architect of this emotionless utopia."

Aria winced at the mention of her mother. "How did you know that?"

Evan shrugged, a fluid movement that seemed to ripple through his entire body. "I make it my business to know things. Especially about the people who try to 'collect' me."

"I'm not-" Aria started, then stopped. Wasn't she? Wasn't that what she had come here to do? "You shouldn't be here," she said instead. "This area is restricted."

"Ah, yes. Can't have people stumbling across remnants of the old world, can we?" Evan gestured around the dilapidated theater. "Might spark a dangerous nostalgia. Or worse, fantasy."

Aria felt a flicker of... something. Annoyance? It had been so long since she'd felt it, she couldn't be sure. "You're breaking at least six different rules just by being here."

"Only six? I must be slipping."

Despite herself, Aria felt the corners of her mouth twitch upward. She forced them back down. "This isn't a joke, Evan. You have to come with us."

Evan's smile faded, replaced by something more serious. "Do I? And what exactly will happen to me if I do? Best case, I'll be locked up and studied like a lab rat. Worst case... well, let's just say I doubt the powers that be would be comfortable with someone they can't control running around."

Aria opened her mouth to protest, to assure him that wasn't true. But the words died in her throat. Because deep down, in a place she rarely acknowledged, she knew he was right.

"Aria," Maya called from behind her, "time's up. We have to call this in."

Evan's eyes locked with Aria's, and she felt as if he could see right through her carefully constructed facade. "You have to make a choice, Collector Thorne. Right here, right now. Are you going to be who they trained you to be, or who you really are?"

Aria's mind raced. This wasn't happening. This couldn't be happening. She was a Collector, one of the best. She had a duty, a purpose. She couldn't just throw that away because of one encounter, one man who stirred up feelings she didn't even understand.

Could she?

"I..." she started, but the words wouldn't come.

"Aria," Maya said again, more insistently this time. "I'm calling it in."

Time seemed to slow down. Aria saw Maya reach for her comm unit. She saw Evan, tense and ready to bolt. And she saw herself, reflected in Evan's eyes, standing at a crossroads she never thought she'd face.

In that moment, Aria made a decision that would change everything.

"Wait!" she shouted, louder than necessary. Maya's hand froze on her device. Evan's eyebrows raised in surprise.

Aria took a deep breath. "He's... he's with me."

Maya's usually impassive face showed obvious confusion. "What?"

"He's part of a... a classified operation," Aria lied, the words tumbling out faster than she could think them through. "Director Kaine personally assigned me. That's why I've been... distracted lately. I wasn't supposed to tell anyone, but..." She gestured helplessly.

For a long moment, no one moved. Aria could feel sweat trickling down her forehead. Then Maya slowly nodded.

"I see," she said, though her tone suggested that she didn't see at all. "I'll... I'll make a note in my report that this area has been cleared."

Aria let out a breath she hadn't realized she was holding. "Thank you, Maya. I owe you one."

As Maya turned to leave, her eyes met Aria's one last time. There was something in them - worry? suspicion? - that made Aria's stomach twist. But then Maya was gone, leaving Aria alone with Evan.

"Well," Evan said, breaking the tense silence, "this was unexpected."

Aria whirled around to face him, her calm facade cracking. "What have you done to me?" she demanded.

Evan held his hands up in a soothing gesture. "I didn't do anything. This was all you, Aria."

"No," she shook her head vehemently. "No, I wouldn't... I didn't..." She trailed off, unable to finish the thought.

Evan came closer, his voice softer. "You made a choice. Maybe the first real choice you've made in years. How does it feel?"

Aria wanted to say that it felt wrong. Scary. Like she was falling without knowing where she was going to land. But what came out instead was, "Alive. It feels... alive."

A genuine smile spread across Evan's face, and Aria felt something warm blossom in her chest. "That's a good start," he said. "Now, what do you say we get out of here before your colleague changes her mind?"

Aria knew she should say no. She should call Maya back, report Evan, go back to her orderly, emotionless life. But as she looked at Evan, at the spark of life in his eyes that she'd never seen in anyone else, she realized she couldn't. Not now that she'd had a taste of... whatever it was.

"Okay," she said, surprising herself. "But I have questions. Lots of questions."

Evan's crooked smile returned. "I'd be disappointed if you didn't. Come on, I know a place where we can talk."

As Aria followed Evan out of the theater and into the fading afternoon light, she felt like she was entering a new world. A world of color and emotion, of danger and possibility.

A world she was suddenly, inexplicably eager to explore.

FOUR
UNDERGROUND CURRENTS

Aria's heart raced as she followed Evan through a maze of narrow alleyways. Every shadow seemed to hide a potential threat, every sound a harbinger of discovery. She'd never been to this part of the city before - a realm of crumbling buildings and faded murals, remnants of a world long suppressed.

"Are you sure you know where you're going?" she hissed, looking nervously over her shoulder.

Evan's laugh was low and warm, sending an unfamiliar chill down her spine. "Trust me, Collector. I could navigate these streets blindfolded."

"Don't call me that," Aria snapped, the title suddenly feeling like a brand. "Not... not anymore."

Evan paused and turned to face her. His eyes seemed to glow in the dim light. "Fair enough. Aria, then."

The way he said her name - softly, almost reverently - made her catch her breath. She pushed the feeling aside and focused on her surroundings. "Where exactly are you taking me?"

"Somewhere safe," Evan replied, resuming their journey. "Somewhere you can get answers to your questions."

They turned a corner and Aria froze. In front of them stood an ancient building, its facade covered in swirling patterns of color. It was like nothing she'd ever seen before, a riot of hues that seemed to pulse with life.

"What is this place?" she breathed, unable to tear her eyes away.

Evan's smile was in his voice. "This, Aria, is what your people would call an emotional center. We call it home."

He placed his hand on a seemingly random part of the mural. To Aria's astonishment, a section of the wall slid open, revealing a hidden passageway.

"After you," Evan gestured, his eyes twinkling with amusement at her shocked expression.

Aria hesitated only a moment before stepping into the unknown. The passage was dark, lit only by strips of soft, pulsing light along the floor. As they descended a spiral staircase, the sounds of muffled voices and unfamiliar music grew louder.

They emerged into a vast underground chamber that took Aria's breath away. The walls were covered with more murals depicting scenes of joy, sorrow, anger, love - the full spectrum of human emotion. People milled about, their faces animated, their voices rising and falling in a cacophony of emotion.

"Welcome," Evan said softly, "to the Sanctuary.

A young woman with vibrant blue hair approached them, her face breaking into a wide grin. "Evan! You're back!" Her eyes landed on Aria and the grin faded. "And you brought a... friend?"

Evan placed a reassuring hand on Aria's shoulder. The touch sent a shock through her body. "It's okay, Zara. She's with me."

Zara's eyes narrowed as she took in Aria's uniform. "She's a collector, Evan. Are you out of your mind?"

"Ex-Collector," Aria found herself saying, surprising even herself. "I... I'm not sure what I am anymore."

Zara's expression softened slightly. "Well, that's a start, I suppose. Come, the others will want to meet you."

As they moved through the crowd, Aria felt overwhelmed. Everywhere she looked, people were openly expressing their emotions - laughing, crying, arguing, hugging. It was beautiful and terrifying at the same time.

They reached a small alcove where a group had gathered around a table. An older man with kind eyes looked up as they approached.

"Evan," he said warmly, "glad you made it back in one piece." His gaze shifted to Aria, and she felt as if he could see right through her. "And who might this be?"

"This is Aria," Evan said, a hint of pride in his voice. "She made a choice today. A brave one."

The older man stood and offered his hand. "Welcome, Aria. I'm David. We've been hoping to meet you for a long time."

Aria hesitantly shook his hand. "You... you have?"

David nodded and gestured for her to sit down. "Indeed. We've been watching you for a while. You're different from the other Gatherers. More... aware."

Aria's mind reeled. "I don't understand. How could you know this? Why me?"

"Because," Evan said gently, sitting down beside her, "you are like us, Aria. You feel things, even if you don't know it yet."

"That's impossible," Aria protested, but even as she said it, she knew it wasn't true. The doubt she had felt, the curiosity, the strange sensations in her chest - they were all emotions, weren't they?

David leaned forward, his voice deep and urgent. "Aria, what do you know about your mother's work? About the true nature of the Emotional Regulation Initiative?"

Aria frowned. "I know what everyone knows. She saved us from chaos, from the empathy pandemic that nearly destroyed society."

Zara scoffed. "They still teach that? Unbelievable."

"Zara," David warned before turning back to Aria. "The truth is more complicated than that. The Initiative didn't just suppress emotions - it transferred them. Your mother found a way to extract emotions from the general population and concentrate them in a select few."

Aria shook her head, unable to process what she was hearing. "No, that's... that's not possible. Why would she do that?"

"Control," Evan said quietly. "A population without emotions is easy to control. And those with the ability to feel, to truly experience the world - they become invaluable. Or dangerous."

"Like you," Aria breathed, looking at Evan with new understanding.

He nodded. "Like me. Like all of us here. And like you, Aria."

"But I'm not... I mean, I'm not..." Aria struggled to find the words.

David reached out and put a comforting hand on hers. "You've suppressed your feelings your whole life, Aria. It will take time for them to fully emerge. But they're there. Your mother made sure of that."

Aria's head spun around. It was too much to take in. Her entire worldview was crumbling around her. "I need... I need a moment."

She stood abruptly, almost knocking over her chair, and stormed out of the alcove. She heard Evan calling after her, but she didn't stop. She pushed through the crowd, desperate for air, for space to think.

She found herself in a small, quiet room off the main chamber. The walls here were bare except for a single mirror. Aria stared at her reflection, searching for some sign of truth in her face.

"It's a lot to take in, isn't it?"

Aria spun around to find Evan standing in the doorway, his expression a mixture of concern and understanding.

"How can you be so calm about this?" she demanded. "If what they're saying is true, then everything I've believed, everything I've done as a Collector... it's all been a lie."

Evan stepped closer, his voice soft. "Not a lie, Aria. A misunderstanding. You did what you thought was right, based on the information you had."

"And now?" Aria asked, her voice barely a whisper. "What am I supposed to do?"

Evan's hand found hers, intertwining their fingers. The touch sent a ripple of warmth through her body. "Now," he said, "you feel. You learn. You're helping us show the world what it's been missing."

Aria looked down at her joined hands, then back up at Evan's face. For the first time, she allowed herself to really see him-the warmth in his eyes, the soft curve of his smile. And for the first time, she allowed herself to feel the flutter in her chest, the quickening of her pulse.

"I'm scared," she admitted, the words foreign on her tongue.

Evan's smile widened. "Good," he said. "That's a perfect place to start."

FIVE
AWAKENING

Aria's hand tingled where Evan had touched it, the sensation both strange and exciting. She flexed her fingers, trying to make sense of the jumble of emotions coursing through her.

"So what happens now?" she asked, her voice barely above a whisper.

Evan's eyes softened. "Well, we're going to help you understand what you're feeling. It'll be overwhelming at first, but..."

A sharp knock on the door interrupted him. Zara's voice came through, tight with urgency. "Evan, we have a situation. The Enforcers are doing a sweep in Sector 7. We need to move."

Evan's expression hardened. He turned to Aria, all business now. "Are you ready for this? Once we leave the Sanctuary, there's no turning back."

Aria's heart raced. Was she ready? Everything was happening so fast. But when she looked at Evan, at the life and emotion in his eyes, she knew she couldn't go back to the cold, sterile world she'd left behind.

"I'm ready," she said, surprised at the firmness in her voice.

Evan nodded, a hint of pride in his smile. "Then let's go."

They followed Zara through a series of winding tunnels, the pulsing lights casting eerie shadows on the walls. Aria's Collector training kicked in, cataloging exits, analyzing potential threats. But now those instincts were tinged with something new - fear, yes, but also excitement.

They emerged into another part of the city, the night air cool on Aria's skin. She could hear the distant whine of Enforcer drones, her nerves on edge.

"We need to split up," Zara said, her eyes scanning the skyline. "Evan, take Aria to the safe house in Sector 9. I'll create a diversion to draw the Enforcers away."

"Zara, no," Evan protested. "It's too dangerous."

Zara's laugh was sharp and bright. "Danger is my middle name, remember? Besides," she added, her expression softening as she looked at Aria, "someone has to make sure our new friend here gets a chance at freedom."

Before Aria could respond, Zara had disappeared into the shadows. The sudden absence of her vibrant presence left an ache in Aria's chest - was this what it felt like to miss someone?

"Come on," Evan said, tugging gently on her arm. "We need to move."

As they walked through the dark streets, Aria's mind raced. "Evan, I don't understand. How can you all feel so... intense? I thought the Initiative affected everyone."

Evan's voice was low as they ducked into an alley. "It did, for the most part. But some of us were born with a natural resistance to it. Others, like you, were... special cases."

"What do you mean, special cases?"

Evan hesitated, then sighed. "Your mother... she made sure you wouldn't be fully affected by the Initiative. She wanted you to have the ability to feel, even if you didn't know how."

Aria stumbled, the revelation hitting her like a physical blow. "She... what? Why would she do that?"

"I don't know exactly," Evan admitted. "But I think, in the end, she couldn't bear to take away her own daughter's humanity."

Aria's mind whirled. All those years of feeling different, of not quite fitting in - had this been the reason? And her mother... had she known all along?

A sudden burst of anger flared in her chest, hot and unfamiliar. "She had no right," Aria hissed. "She took emotions from everyone else, but decided I should be different? Who gave her that choice?"

Evan stopped and turned to face her. His eyes were filled with a mixture of concern and... was that admiration? "Aria, I know this is a lot to process. But right now we need to focus on getting to safety. Can you do that?"

Aria took a deep breath and tried to center herself. The anger was still there, simmering beneath the surface, but she nodded. "Yes. I can."

They walked on, the streets getting quieter as they entered Sector 9. Aria recognized this area - she had patrolled it countless times as a Collector. Now, seeing it with new eyes, she noticed details she'd missed before. The way some windows glowed with a warmer light than others. The subtle variations in the supposedly uniform architecture.

"Here," Evan said, stopping in front of a nondescript building. He placed his hand on a hidden panel and a door slid silently open.

Inside, the safe house was sparse but comfortable. Evan quickly secured the entrance while Aria took in her surroundings. A worn couch, a small kitchenette, a bookshelf filled with actual paper books - relics from the old world.

"We should be safe here for now," Evan said, turning back to her. "How are you holding up?"

Aria sank onto the couch, suddenly exhausted. "I don't know. I feel... everything. It's like I've been asleep my whole life and now I'm awake and the world is too bright, too loud."

Evan sat next to her, close enough that she could feel the warmth radiating from his body. "That's normal. It'll take some time to adjust. But, Aria," he added, his voice softening, "you're doing amazingly well. Most people who've been emotionally repressed for so long... they break when the feelings come back. You're embracing it."

Aria looked at him, really looked. The seriousness in his eyes, the soft curve of his lips, the way his presence made her feel both calm and exhilarated. Without thinking, she reached out and brushed her fingers across his cheek.

Evan's breath caught and his eyes widened in surprise. "Aria..."

"I want to understand," she whispered. "All of it. The good, the bad, everything I've missed."

For a moment, they stayed like that, suspended in a bubble of possibility. Then, slowly, cautiously, Evan leaned in. His lips met hers, soft and warm, and Aria felt her world explode in color.

The kiss was gentle, exploratory, but it awakened something in Aria she never knew existed. When they finally pulled apart, both breathless, she felt dizzy with the sensation.

"That," Evan said, his voice hoarse, "was joy. And attraction. And about a dozen other emotions I don't think you have names for yet."

Aria touched her lips, still tingling from the kiss. "Is it always like this?"

Evan's laugh was deep and warm. "No, it's not always like this. Sometimes it's better. Sometimes it hurts. But that's the beauty of it, Aria. Feeling everything, the good and the bad, is what makes us human."

As they sat there, the reality of their situation slowly seeped back in. They were fugitives now, hunted by the very system Aria had once served. But looking at Evan, feeling the warmth of his hand in hers, Aria knew she'd made the right choice.

Whatever came next, whatever challenges they faced, she was ready to face them. Ready to feel them with every newly awakened fiber of her being.

SIX
ECHOES OF THE PAST

Aria jerked awake, her heart pounding. For a moment she didn't know where she was. The soft light filtering through unfamiliar curtains, the worn couch beneath her - everything felt wrong.

Then she remembered. The sanctuary. Evan. The kiss.

She sat up and ran a hand through her tangled hair. Evan was nowhere to be seen, but she could hear soft movement in the small kitchen area.

"Evan?" she called, her voice still hoarse from sleep.

He appeared in the doorway, a steaming mug in each hand. The sight of him - tousled hair, kind eyes, gentle smile - made her heart flutter.

"Morning," he said, offering her one of the mugs. "I hope you like tea. It's all we have here."

Aria took the cup and inhaled the unfamiliar aroma. "I've never had tea before," she admitted. "The Nutrition Center always said it was an unnecessary indulgence."

Evan's laugh was warm and rich. "Well, prepare for your first unnecessary indulgence of many."

As Aria sipped the tea - bitter at first, then surprisingly comforting - Evan settled down beside her on the couch. The closeness sent a shiver down her spine.

"How are you feeling?" he asked, his eyes searching her face.

Aria considered the question. How did she feel? The word itself was so new, so strange. "Overwhelmed," she finally said. "Like I'm standing on the edge of a cliff and I don't know if I'm going to fall or fly."

Evan nodded, understanding in his eyes. "That's normal. It's a lot to process. But Aria," he added, his voice softening, "you're not in this alone. We're all here to help you deal with these new feelings."

A lump formed in Aria's throat. She swallowed hard, trying to identify the emotion. Gratitude? Fear? Both?

Before she could answer, a sharp knock on the door made them both jump. Evan was on his feet in an instant, his body tense.

"Stay here," he whispered, moving silently towards the entrance.

Aria's heart pounded as Evan peered through the peephole. Then, to her surprise, his shoulders relaxed.

"It's okay," he called back to her. "It's David."

The door opened to reveal the older man from the Sanctuary, his kind eyes now clouded with concern.

"We have a problem," David said without preamble. "The Enforcers are widening their search. They know we're hiding someone important."

Evan's brow furrowed. "How? We were being careful."

David's eyes shifted to Aria. "Because they're not looking for just any defector. They're looking for her. Aria Thorne, daughter of Dr. Elena Thorne."

Aria felt as if the floor had been pulled out from under her. "What? But how could they know that?"

"Because," a new voice said, "I told them."

Aria spun around to see Maya standing in the doorway, her Collector uniform pristine, her face a mask of calm determination.

"Maya?" Aria breathed, disbelief and betrayal fighting inside her. "How did you..."

"Find you?" Maya finished, stepping into the room. "I followed you, of course. After your strange behavior at the theater, I knew something was wrong. I had to make sure you weren't... compromised."

Evan moved to stand between Maya and Aria, his posture protective. "And now what? You're here to bring her back?"

Maya's eyes flickered with something - regret? Fear? "I'm here to save her," she said. "Aria, please. Come back with me. Tell them you were undercover, gathering information on the Resistance. It's not too late."

Aria stared at her former colleague, this woman she'd worked with for years. Had there always been this depth of feeling behind Maya's impassive facade?

"Maya," Aria said quietly, "I can't go back. Not now that I know the truth. About the Initiative, about my mother, about... everything."

Maya's composure broke, just for a moment. "Aria, please.

You don't understand. If you don't come back willingly, they'll-"

A sudden explosion shook the building, cutting off Maya's words. Dust rained down from the ceiling as alarms blared in the distance.

"They're here," David said grimly. "We have to move. Now."

Evan grabbed Aria's hand and pulled her toward a hidden panel in the wall. "There's a tunnel system," he explained quickly. "It will lead us to another safe house."

Aria hesitated and looked back at Maya. "Come with us," she pleaded. "You feel it too, don't you? The wrongness of it all?"

For a moment, Maya looked torn. Then her face hardened. "I'm sorry, Aria. I really am."

As Maya reached for her communication device, David moved with surprising speed. His hand connected with Maya's neck, and she crumpled to the floor.

"She'll be fine," David assured Aria, seeing her shocked expression. "But we have to go. Now."

As they hurried into the dark tunnel, the sounds of the Enforcer drones growing louder behind them, Aria's mind raced. Maya's betrayal, the Enforcers' pursuit, the growing realization that her entire life had been built on lies - it all swirled together in a maelstrom of emotions she couldn't begin to untangle.

But Evan's hand was warm in hers, a lifeline in the chaos. And as they ran through the darkness, Aria made a silent vow. She would uncover the truth about her mother's work, about the true purpose of the Initiative. And somehow, someway, she would set things right.

The tunnel stretched before her, dark and uncertain. But for the first time in her life, Aria embraced the unknown, ready to feel whatever came next - fear, hope, and everything in between.

SEVEN

BENEATH THE SURFACE

The tunnel seemed endless, a twisting maze of darkness and echoes. Aria's lungs burned as they ran, Evan's hand still clenched tightly in hers. Behind them, the sounds of pursuit had faded, but the fear remained, a constant presence at the back of her mind.

Finally, Evan slowed down, his breathing ragged. "We should be safe here for now," he panted, leaning against the damp wall.

Aria doubled over, hands on her knees, gulping for air. As her heartbeat began to calm, other sensations crept in. The chill of the tunnel. The musty smell of earth and ancient stone. The way her body was shaking, not just from exertion, but from a cocktail of emotions she couldn't even begin to name.

"Are you okay?" Evan asked, his voice low with concern.

Aria straightened, meeting his gaze in the dim emergency lighting. "I don't know," she admitted. "I feel... everything. It's overwhelming."

Evan's smile was tinged with sadness. "That's the thing about feelings, Aria. They don't always make sense. But they're real, and they're yours."

A lump formed in Aria's throat. "Even the bad ones?"

"Especially the bad ones," Evan said, reaching out to brush a tear from her cheek. Aria hadn't even noticed she was crying. "They're part of what makes us human."

For a moment they stood in silence, the weight of everything that had happened settling over them. Then David's voice echoed from further down the tunnel.

"We need to keep moving," he called. "There's a safe room not far from here."

As they started walking again, Aria's mind raced. "David," she said, "how did you know about these tunnels? How long has this been going on?"

David's chuckle was deep and rueful. "Longer than you think, my dear. These tunnels were built long before the Initiative, by people who feared a different kind of oppression. We just... repurposed them."

"And the Resistance?" Aria pressed. "How many of you are there?"

"More than the Council knows," Evan replied. "But not enough. Not yet."

They rounded a corner and David held up a hand, signaling them to stop. He ran his fingers along the wall until he found what he was looking for - a small, almost invisible panel. A moment later, a section of the wall slid open, revealing a hidden room.

Inside, the room was small, but well equipped. Monitors lined one wall, showing various parts of the city. A small kitchenette occupied another corner, while cots and storage containers filled the rest of the room.

"Welcome to Control," David said, a note of pride in his voice. "This is where we coordinate all Resistance activities in the eastern sectors."

Aria stared at the monitors, recognizing streets and buildings she'd patrolled countless times as a Collector. How much had happened right under her nose?

"Aria," Evan said gently, "I know this is a lot to take in. But we need to know what you can tell us about the Initiative. About your mother's work."

Aria tore her eyes from the screens and met Evan's serious gaze. "I... I don't know much," she admitted. "Only what everyone knows. That it was designed to save us from the empathy pandemic, to create a stable society."

David shook his head, his expression grim. "That's the official story. The reality is much darker."

He tapped a few keys on a nearby console, and one of the screens changed to show a familiar face. Aria's breath caught in her throat.

"Mom?" she whispered.

The image was of a younger Dr. Elena Thorne, her face animated as she spoke to someone off screen. There was no sound, but Aria could see the passion in her mother's eyes, so at odds with the calm, unemotional demeanor she remembered.

"This was taken just before the Initiative was implemented," David explained. "Your mother was brilliant, Aria. But she was also afraid. Afraid of what unchecked emotions could do to humanity."

"So she decided to take them away?" Aria asked, unable to keep the bitterness out of her voice.

"Not exactly," Evan said. "The Initiative doesn't just suppress emotions. It... redirects them."

Aria frowned. "What do you mean?"

David sighed heavily. "The emotions aren't gone, Aria. They're stored. Collected. In people like you."

The words hit Aria like a physical blow. She stumbled back, her mind reeling. "That's... that's not possible. I don't--"

But even as she denied it, a part of her knew it was true. The strange sensations she'd always felt during extractions, the way she'd always been different from other Collectors... it all made a terrible kind of sense.

"Why?" she choked out. "Why would she do this?"

"Control," Evan said quietly. "A population without emotions is easy to control. And those who can feel, who can experience the full range of human emotion..."

"They become invaluable," Aria finished, the realization dawning. "Or dangerous."

David nodded grimly. "Exactly. Your mother thought she was saving humanity. Instead, she created a system of emotional slavery."

Aria's legs gave out and she sank to the floor, her head in her hands. It was too much. The weight of it all - the lies, the betrayal, the enormity of what had been done - threatened to crush her.

She felt Evan kneel beside her, his hand warm on her back. "Aria," he said softly, "I know it's overwhelming. But you're not alone in this. And you have a power that can change everything."

Aria looked up and met his gaze. "What do you mean?"

Evan's eyes were intense, filled with a mixture of hope and determination. "You're not just a Gatherer, Aria. You're a conduit. You can absorb emotions, yes, but you can also give them back. You could be the key to awakening people, to showing them what they've lost."

The idea was both terrifying and exhilarating. Aria thought of Maya, of the glimmer of emotion she'd seen in her former colleague's eyes. Could she really help people feel again?

As if reading her thoughts, David spoke. "It won't be easy. The Council will do everything in its power to stop us. But if we can show people the truth, if we can help them feel again..."

"We could change everything," Aria finished, a newfound determination strengthening her voice.

She stood, her legs shaky but her mind firm. Looking from Evan to David, she saw hope reflected in their eyes. Hope, and something more. Faith. Faith in her.

For the first time since this all began, Aria felt a new emotion blossom in her chest. It was warm and bright, filling her with a strength she'd never known before.

It was purpose.

"Okay," she said, her voice calm. "Where do we start?"

EIGHT

THE FIRST AWAKENING

A ria stared at her reflection in the small, cracked mirror. The face looking back at her was familiar, yet somehow strange. Her eyes, once a cool, emotionless gray, now seemed to shimmer with depth and life.

"Are you ready?" Evan's voice came from behind her, soft and encouraging.

Aria took a deep breath, steadying herself. "As ready as I'll ever be, I suppose."

It had been three days since their escape, three days of intense preparation and planning. Now the moment of truth had arrived. They were about to attempt their first "awakening" - using Aria's newfound abilities to restore emotions to someone under the influence of the Initiative.

David appeared in the doorway, his face etched with concern. "Remember, Aria, this is just a test. If anything feels wrong, stop immediately. Understood?"

Aria nodded, grateful for his fatherly concern. It was a new feeling to have someone so openly concerned about her well-being. "I understand, David. I'll be careful."

They made their way to the main area of the safe house, where a nervous-looking young man was waiting. Zara stood beside him, her usual bravado tempered by the gravity of the situation.

"Aria, this is Tom," Zara introduced. "He's been with the Resistance for about a year now, but he's never... felt before. Not really."

Tom's eyes met Aria's, and she saw a flicker of something - hope, perhaps? "I'm ready," he said, his voice steady despite his obvious fear.

Aria approached him slowly, her heart pounding. She'd spent the last few days learning to control her abilities, to channel the vast well of emotions within her. But this would be the first time she would try to give those emotions to someone else.

"It may feel strange at first," she warned Tom. "If it becomes too much, just say the word and we'll stop."

Tom nodded and squared his shoulders. "I trust you."

Aria reached out and placed her hands on either side of Tom's face. She closed her eyes and focused on the swirling emotions inside her. Joy, fear, anger, love - they all danced beneath her skin, waiting to be released.

Slowly, carefully, she let them flow. She thought of the happiness she'd felt when Evan kissed her, the wonder of seeing color for the first time, the warmth of friendship with Zara and David. She channeled those feelings and pushed them gently towards Tom.

At first, nothing seemed to happen. Then, suddenly, Tom gasped. His eyes widened and filled with tears.

"Oh," he breathed, his voice filled with awe. "Oh, I... I feel..."

Aria opened her eyes, keeping the connection. Tom's face was a canvas of emotions - joy and fear, confusion and elation, all vying for dominance.

"That's it," Aria encouraged, her own eyes stinging with unshed tears. "Let it come."

Tom laughed, the sound bright and uninhibited. Then, just as quickly, he was sobbing, great heaving cries that shook his entire body. Aria held on, guiding him through the storm of emotions.

After what seemed like hours, but was probably only minutes, Tom's emotional storm began to calm. Aria gently broke the connection and stepped back. Tom swayed on his feet and Zara quickly moved to support him.

"How are you feeling?" Aria asked softly, her hands shaking slightly as she lowered them.

Tom blinked quickly, his eyes darting around the room as if he were seeing it for the first time. "I... I don't know," he said, his voice thick with emotion. "Everything is so... intense. So vivid."

Zara squeezed his shoulder, her own eyes glistening. "Take your time, Tom. It's a lot to take in."

Tom nodded, then suddenly broke into a wide, genuine smile. "I feel... alive," he said, wonder evident in his voice. "For the first time, I really feel alive."

The room let out a collective exhale, a tension Aria hadn't even realized was there suddenly dissipating. Evan moved to her side, his hand finding hers and squeezing gently.

"You did it," he whispered, pride in his voice.

Aria leaned against him, suddenly exhausted. The emotional transfer had taken more out of her than she'd expected. "We did it," she corrected, offering him a weary smile.

David approached Tom, his expression a mixture of joy and scientific curiosity. "Tom, can you describe what you're experiencing? Any physical sensations along with the emotions?"

Tom nodded eagerly, the words coming out in a rush. "It's like... like I've been seeing the world in black and white, and suddenly everything is in color. My heart beats faster, my skin feels more sensitive. And inside..." He put a hand on his chest. "Inside, it's like there's this warm, glowing ball of... of everything."

As Tom continued to describe his experience, Aria felt a wave of dizziness wash over her. She swayed slightly, and Evan's arm immediately went around her waist, steadying her.

"Aria?" he asked, concern written all over his face. "Are you okay?"

She nodded, trying to shake off the tiredness. "Just tired, I guess. It took more energy than I thought it would."

David was at her side in an instant, his clinical eye assessing her. "We should get you to bed. You need to rest."

Aria wanted to protest, to stay and watch Tom's continued awakening, but her body betrayed her. Her knees buckled, and only Evan's quick reflexes kept her from falling.

"Okay, that's enough for today," Evan said firmly, scooping her into his arms. Aria was too exhausted to be embarrassed by the gesture.

As Evan carried her into the small bedroom, Aria's mind raced despite her fatigue. They'd done it. They'd actually awakened someone. It was proof that their abilities could make a difference, that they had a real chance to change things.

Evan gently laid her down on the bed and pulled a blanket over her. "Rest," he said softly, brushing a strand of hair from her face. "We can talk more when you wake up."

Aria caught his hand as he turned to leave. "Evan," she said, her voice barely above a whisper. "We really did it, didn't we? We can really change things."

Evan's smile was warm, his eyes shining with an emotion Aria was just beginning to understand. "We did," he confirmed. "And this is just the beginning."

As sleep began to claim her, Aria's last conscious thought was of the future stretching out before them. A future full of color, of emotion, of life. It was terrifying and exhilarating and absolutely worth fighting for.

In the other room she could hear Tom's laughter, bright and uninhibited. It was the sound of a world beginning to awaken, one person at a time. And Aria was the key to it all.

Her dreams, when they came, were vivid and intense - full of swirling colors and powerful emotions. For the first time in her life, Aria welcomed them, embracing the chaos and beauty of a fully felt existence.

Hours later, Aria awoke to the soft sound of voices. She lay still for a moment, allowing her senses to adjust. The emotional fatigue had mostly faded, replaced by a throbbing energy that seemed to run through her veins.

Slowly, she sat up and swung her legs over the side of the bed. Her body felt different somehow - more alive, more present. Was this how Tom felt? Was this how everyone would feel when they woke up?

She made her way to the door, pausing when she recognized Evan and David's voices in a low conversation.

"...risks we have to consider," David said, his tone serious. "The more people we wake, the more attention we'll draw."

"I know," Evan replied, a hint of frustration in his voice. "But you saw what happened to Tom. We can't just sit on this, David. People deserve to know, to feel."

"And they will," David assured him. "But we have to be strategic. When the Council realizes what Aria can do..."

"They'll stop at nothing to get her back," Evan finished grimly.

Aria's breath caught in her throat. She knew, logically, that she was in danger. But hearing it so bluntly made it real in a way it hadn't been before.

Taking a deep breath, she pushed the door open and stepped into the room. Evan and David turned to her, their conversation coming to an abrupt halt.

"Aria," Evan said, moving to her side. "How are you feeling?"

She offered him a small smile. "Better. Stronger." She looked between him and David. "And ready to face whatever comes next."

David's expression softened. "You heard us, didn't you?"

Aria nodded. "I did. And I understand the risks. But I also understand what's at stake." She straightened her shoulders, feeling a newfound determination coursing through her. "I want to keep going. I want to wake up more people."

Evan and David exchanged a look, a silent communication passing between them. Finally, David nodded.

"All right," he said. "But we do this carefully. We make a plan, we move slowly, and at the first sign of trouble, we pull out. Agreed?"

Aria nodded firmly. "Agreed."

As they began to discuss strategy, Aria felt a flutter of excitement in her chest. They were on the verge of something monumental, something that could change the very fabric of their society.

It would be dangerous. It would be difficult. But when Aria looked at Evan, saw the passion and determination in his eyes, she knew it would be worth it.

They would wake up the world, one heart at a time. And Aria was ready for whatever challenges lay ahead.

NINE
RIPPLES IN THE POND

Aria's fingers trembled as she adjusted the collar of her borrowed clothing. The fabric felt strange against her skin, so different from the crisp uniformity of her Collector garb. She stared at her reflection in the cracked mirror, barely recognizing the woman looking back at her.

"Are you ready for this?" Evan's voice came from behind her, a mixture of concern and encouragement.

Aria took a deep breath and steadied herself. "As ready as I'll ever be, I guess."

Two weeks had passed since Tom's awakening. Two weeks of planning, preparing and practicing. Now they were about to venture into the city for the first time since their escape. The plan was simple, yet terrifying: find someone receptive to awakening and bring them back to the safe house.

Evan's hand found hers, warm and reassuring. "Remember, we're just scouting today. No pressure to make contact unless you're absolutely sure."

Aria nodded, grateful for his constant presence. As they made their way to the main room, she could feel the nervous energy radiating from the others. Zara was pacing, her usual bravado tempered by obvious anxiety. David sat at the console, his fingers flying over the keys as he made last-minute adjustments to their security protocols.

Tom, still adjusting to his newfound emotions, offered Aria a shaky smile. "Good luck out there," he said, his voice thick with emotion. "What you're doing... it's incredible."

A lump formed in Aria's throat. She still wasn't used to such open displays of emotion. "Thank you, Tom. We'll be careful."

David turned away from the console, his face etched with concern. "Remember, if anything feels wrong, abort immediately. No heroics."

"We know, David," Evan said, a hint of loving desperation in his voice. "We'll be back before you know it."

As they prepared to leave, Zara pulled Aria into a fierce embrace. The physical contact, once so strange, now felt comforting. "Give them hell, girl," Zara whispered.

With final nods to their friends, Aria and Evan stepped into the tunnel that would lead them back to the city above. As they walked, Aria's mind raced. What if they were caught? What if she couldn't control her powers? What if...

"Hey," Evan's voice cut through her swirling thoughts. "You can do this, Aria. I believe in you."

His words settled over her like a warm blanket, calming her frayed nerves. She squeezed his hand in silent thanks.

They emerged into a quiet alley, the late afternoon sun casting long shadows. Aria blinked, her eyes adjusting to the natural light. The city looked different somehow, as if she was seeing it for the first time.

"Where to first?" she asked, trying to keep her voice steady.

Evan consulted a small device on his wrist. "There's a park about two blocks from here. It's usually crowded this time of day. Good place to watch without drawing attention."

They made their way through the streets, Aria hyper-aware of every passing face, every potential threat. But no one gave them a second glance. They were just two more citizens going about their day.

The park was indeed busy, filled with people enjoying the pleasant weather. Couples walked hand in hand, their faces calm. Children played on the equipment, their movements efficient but cheerless. It was a scene of perfect order, and it made Aria's skin crawl.

They found a bench and sat down, trying to look casual. Aria let her eyes wander, reaching out with her newfound empathic senses. Most of the people she touched felt... muted. Like radio static where there should be music.

But then something caught her eye. A young woman sitting alone by the fountain, her fingers tracing patterns in the water. There was something different about her, a flicker of... something.

"Evan," Aria whispered, nodding subtly to the woman. "I think I feel something."

Evan followed her gaze, his body tensing slightly. "Are you sure?"

Aria nodded, her pulse quickening. "It's faint, but it's there. Like... like an echo of emotion."

They watched the woman for several minutes, debating their next move. Just as Aria was about to suggest they approach her, a commotion at the park entrance caught their attention.

Aria's blood ran cold. Enforcers. A full squad, moving through the crowd with purposeful strides.

"We have to go," Evan said urgently, already standing. "Now."

But it was too late. One of the Enforcers had spotted them, his eyes widening in recognition. "There!" he shouted, pointing in their direction. "Collector Thorne!"

Panic rushed through Aria, sharp and overwhelming. She felt frozen, rooted to the spot as the Enforcers advanced.

Evan's hand closed around her arm, pulling her to her feet. "Run!" he hissed.

And then they ran, pushing through the crowd, their hearts pounding in their ears. Aria could hear shouts behind them, the heavy footsteps of pursuit.

They darted down a side street, then another, Evan leading them through a maze of alleys and side streets. Aria's lungs burned, her legs ached, but fear kept her moving.

Finally, after what felt like hours but was probably only minutes, Evan pulled her into a narrow space between two buildings. They pressed against the wall, trying to calm their ragged breathing.

Footsteps approached, slowed, then passed. Aria held her breath, sure the pounding of her heart would give them away. But the footsteps faded, and silence fell over them.

"I think we lost them," Evan whispered, his voice barely audible.

Aria nodded, not daring to speak. The adrenaline was wearing off, leaving her shaky and nauseous. She slid down the wall, her legs giving out under her.

Evan crouched beside her, concern etched into his face. "Are you okay?"

A hysterical laugh bubbled up from Aria's throat. "Okay? I don't... I don't know what okay is anymore." She looked up at him, tears stinging her eyes. "They knew, Evan. They were looking for me specifically. How did they know?"

Evan's expression darkened. "I don't know. But we'll find out." He helped her to her feet, his touch gentle. "For now, we need to get back to the safe house. Regroup, come up with a new plan."

As they made their way back through the winding alleys, Aria's mind whirled. The woman at the fountain, the one who'd shown a glimmer of emotion - was she okay? Had the Enforcers noticed her, too?

And more importantly, how had they known to look for Aria? The implications were frightening. If they knew she was with the Resistance, what else did they know?

One thing was clear: their task had just become infinitely more complicated. But when Aria looked at Evan, saw the determination in his eyes, she felt a flicker of hope. They'd faced challenges before. They'd face this one, too.

Together.

TEN
SHADOWS AND LIGHT

The safe house was abuzz with activity when Aria and Evan returned. David paced anxiously, his usual calm demeanor shattered. Zara was at the console, fingers flying over the keys as she scanned the security feeds.

"Thank God," David breathed as they stumbled in. "We saw the Enforcer alert go off. What happened?"

Evan quickly recounted their close call in the park. The atmosphere in the room grew heavier with each word.

"This changes everything," David said, running a hand through his gray hair. "If they're actively hunting Aria..."

"We have to move," Zara finished, her voice grim. "This safe house is compromised."

Aria sank into a chair, her legs still shaking from their narrow escape. "I don't understand," she said, frustration bleeding into her voice. "How did they know to come looking for me? And why now?"

A tense silence fell over the room. It was Tom who finally broke it, his voice soft but firm. "It could be my fault."

All eyes turned to him. Tom swallowed hard, then continued. "After... after you woke me up, I felt everything so intensely. I thought I was hiding it well, but..." He trailed off, his eyes downcast.

"Someone noticed," Evan finished, realization dawning on his face.

Tom nodded miserably. "My neighbor. She's a low-level administrator at the Emotional Regulation Center. I think... I think she reported me."

Aria's heart sank. Of course. They'd been so focused on the joy of Tom's awakening that they hadn't considered the ripple effect it might have.

"It's not your fault, Tom," she said, trying to infuse her voice with a confidence she didn't quite feel. "We all underestimated the risks."

David nodded in agreement. "Aria's right. But that means we have to be even more careful going forward." He turned to Zara. "How soon can we be ready to move?"

Zara's brow furrowed in concentration. "Give me an hour to scrub our digital footprint and pack the essentials. We should be able to reach the safe house by nightfall."

As the others bustled about, preparing for their hasty departure, Aria found herself drawn to the small window overlooking the street. The world outside looked so normal, so peaceful. How many people out there were like the woman in the park, harboring tiny sparks of emotion without even realizing it?

She felt Evan's presence before he spoke, a warmth at her back that had become comfortingly familiar. "Credit for your thoughts?" he asked quietly.

Aria turned to face him, struck again by the depth of emotion in his eyes. How had she ever thought the blank stares of her fellow Collectors were normal?

"I was just thinking," she said, "about all the people out there. How many of them might be ready to wake up, if only given the chance?"

Evan's expression softened. "That's why we do this, Aria. To give them that chance."

She nodded, a determination settling over her. "You're right. And we can't give up now, no matter how dangerous it gets."

A smile tugged at Evan's lips. "That's my girl," he said, the words sending a pleasant shiver through her.

Their moment was interrupted by Zara's sharp voice. "Guys, we have a problem."

They hurried over to the console where Zara was pointing to a series of blinking dots on a map of the city. "Enforcer patrols," she explained grimly. "They're setting up checkpoints all over the sector. If we wait much longer, we'll be trapped."

David's face was ashen. "We have to split up. It's too risky to move as a group."

"I'll go first," Evan volunteered immediately. "Check out the route, make sure it's clear."

Aria's chest tightened at the thought of Evan out there alone. "No," she said firmly. "We'll go together."

Evan opened his mouth to argue, but something in Aria's expression stopped him. After a moment, he nodded. "Together, then."

The next few minutes were a blur of hasty preparations. Backpacks were filled with supplies, routes were memorized, final instructions were given.

As Aria and Evan prepared to leave, Tom approached them. His eyes were bright with unshed tears. "I'm sorry," he said, his voice choked with emotion. "I never meant for you to be in danger."

Aria felt a surge of affection for this man, so new to his emotions and yet so deeply felt. Without hesitation, she pulled him into an embrace. "You have nothing to be sorry for," she whispered softly. "We'll get through this, all of us."

With one last hug and whispered good luck, Aria and Evan slipped out into the gathering dusk. The streets were eerily quiet, the usual pedestrian traffic conspicuously absent.

They moved quickly but cautiously, sticking to shadows and back alleys. Aria's every sense was on high alert, her newfound empathic abilities reaching out, searching for any hint of danger.

They were halfway to the rendezvous point when Aria felt it - a surge of cold determination that didn't belong to either of them. She grabbed Evan's arm and pulled him into a doorway just as an Enforcer patrol rounded the corner.

They pressed against the wall, barely daring to breathe. Aria could feel the Enforcers' emotional signatures coming closer, closer...

And then, miraculously, they passed. Aria let out a shaky breath, her heart pounding so hard she was sure it would give them away.

Evan squeezed her hand, a silent question in his eyes. She nodded and they moved on.

The rest of the journey was a tense blur of near misses and silent prayers. By the time they reached the new safe house - a seemingly abandoned warehouse on the outskirts of town - Aria felt as if she had aged years in a matter of hours.

Zara was already there, her relief palpable as she ushered them inside. "David and Tom?" Aria asked immediately.

"Not here yet," Zara replied, her voice strained with worry. "But they've got another hour before we should really start panicking."

As they settled in to wait, Aria found herself drawn to a dirty window overlooking the city. The lights of the Emotional Regulation Center glowed in the distance, a beacon of the very system they were fighting.

She felt Evan's presence beside her, a silent comfort in the growing darkness. "We're really doing this, aren't we?" she asked quietly. "Trying to change everything."

Evan's hand found hers, their fingers intertwined. "We are," he confirmed. "It won't be easy, and it won't be quick. But Aria," he turned her gently to face him, his eyes intense in the dim light, "I believe we can do this. Together."

As Aria looked into Evan's eyes, she felt a surge of emotion so strong it took her breath away. Fear, yes, and uncertainty. But also hope, determination, and something else - something warm and bright and terrifyingly wonderful.

She leaned in, drawn by a force she couldn't name, and Evan met her halfway. Their kiss was soft at first, then deeper, a promise and a declaration all at once.

When they finally parted, both slightly breathless, Aria felt as if something fundamental had changed. The world was still dangerous, her future uncertain. But in this moment, with Evan at her side and the taste of possibility on her lips, Aria knew one thing for certain.

Whatever came next, they would face it together. And that was worth fighting for.

ELEVEN
ECHOES OF THE PAST

Aria jerked awake, her heart pounding. For a moment, she didn't know where she was. The unfamiliar shadows of the warehouse loomed around her, and panic clawed at her throat.

Then she felt Evan's warmth beside her, heard his steady breathing, and reality slowly seeped back in. They were safe. For now.

She sat up carefully, trying not to wake him. The events of the previous day came flooding back - the close call in the park, the frantic escape, the kiss. Her lips tingled at the memory, a flutter of warmth in her chest.

"Aria?" Evan's voice was thick with sleep. "Are you okay?"

She turned to him, drinking in the sight of his disheveled hair and worried eyes. "Just a dream," she whispered. "Go back to sleep."

But Evan was already sitting up, fully alert now. "Do you want to talk about it?"

Aria hesitated. The dream was already fading, leaving only a lingering sense of unease. "It was about my mother," she said slowly. "I think... I think I remembered something."

Evan's brow furrowed. "About the Initiative?"

She nodded, closing her eyes to focus on the fragmented images. "We were in their lab. I was young, maybe five or six. She was... crying." The realization hit her like a physical blow. "I'd never seen her cry before."

Evan's hand found hers, warm and comforting. "What else do you remember?"

Aria's frown deepened as she struggled to piece together the memory. "She said something about a mistake. That she'd gone too far. And then..." She trailed off, frustration bubbling to the surface. "That's all. I don't remember anything else."

"Hey," Evan said quietly, tilting her chin up to meet his gaze. "It's okay. Memories like that, they come back in pieces. Give it time."

Aria nodded, grateful for his understanding. But the unease lingered. What had her mother meant? What mistake?

A noise from across the camp interrupted her thoughts. David and Tom were stirring, and Zara was already at the makeshift command center, fingers flying over a keyboard.

"Morning, lovebirds," Zara called out, a hint of teasing in her voice. "Sleep well?"

Aria felt heat rise in her cheeks, but Evan just chuckled. "As well as can be expected in a warehouse. Any news?"

Zara's expression turned serious. "Actually, yes. And you're not going to like it."

They gathered around the console, tension in the air. Zara pulled up a series of news reports and official bulletins. "They're implementing new emotional screening protocols citywide," she explained grimly. "Mandatory testing for all citizens, effective immediately."

David cursed under his breath. "They're looking for more awakened individuals."

Aria's stomach churned. "It's because of me, isn't it? Because they know I can awaken people."

"It's not your fault," Evan said firmly. "They were always going to escalate eventually. We just have to adjust our plans."

Tom spoke up, his voice trembling but determined. "What if... what if I turned myself in?"

All eyes turned to him in shock. "Absolutely not," David said immediately.

But Tom continued. "Think about it. If I go in, claim I had a momentary lapse but I'm better now, maybe I can throw them off the scent. Buy us some time."

Aria's heart ached at the thought of Tom sacrificing himself. "It's too dangerous," she argued. "We don't know what they might do to you."

"She's right," Evan added. "We stick together. Nobody sacrifices themselves."

They spent the next hour debating strategy, tensions running high as fatigue and fear took their toll. Finally, David raised his hand for silence.

"We're all exhausted and nervous," he said, his voice tired but kind. "Let's take a break, get something to eat, and look at this with fresh eyes."

As they dispersed to their various tasks, Aria found herself drawn back to the window overlooking the city. The Emotional Regulation Center loomed in the distance, a constant reminder of what they were up against.

She felt Evan's presence before he spoke, a warmth at her back that had become painfully familiar. "Credit for your thoughts?" he asked quietly.

Aria turned to face him, struck again by the depth of emotion in his eyes. "I was thinking about my mother," she admitted. "About the dream."

Evan nodded encouragingly. "Did you remember anything else?"

She shook her head, frustration evident in her voice. "No, but... Evan, what if she knew? What if she realized that the Initiative was wrong and tried to stop it?"

"It's possible," Evan said cautiously. "But Aria, we can't base our plans on maybes and what-ifs. We need solid information."

Aria's mind raced. "What if we could get that information? My mother's old lab, maybe it still exists. If we could get in there, we might find some answers."

Evan's eyes widened. "Aria, that's... that's incredibly risky. The lab would be in the heart of the Emotional Regulation Center. It's practically a fortress."

"I know," Aria said, a spark of determination igniting within her. "But I also know the layout, the security protocols. I was a Collector, remember? I can get us in."

Evan studied her face, the conflict clear in his expression. Finally, he sighed. "We'd have to check with the others. And we'd need a solid plan."

Aria nodded eagerly. "Of course. But Evan, think about it. If we could find proof that the Initiative was flawed from the beginning, proof from its own creator... we could change everything."

As they turned back to the others to present their idea, Aria felt a mixture of fear and exhilaration coursing through her veins. It was dangerous, maybe even foolish. But for the first time since this all began, she felt like she had a purpose beyond just running and hiding.

She was going to find out the truth about her mother's work. And maybe, just maybe, she'd find the key to bringing down the entire system.

The others listened in stunned silence as Aria and Evan laid out their plan. By the time they finished, the warehouse was quiet enough to hear a pin drop.

Finally, David spoke, his voice carefully neutral. "It's risky. Incredibly so."

"But it could work," Zara chimed in, a hint of excitement in her tone. "With Aria's inside knowledge and our technology, we could actually pull this off."

Tom nodded vigorously. "Better than sitting here waiting to be found. I say we do it."

All eyes turned to David. He looked at each of them in turn, his expression unreadable. Then he nodded with a heavy sigh. "All right. Let's plan this thing properly. We only have one shot at this and we can't afford to waste it."

As they huddled around the console and began to work out the details of their daring plan, Aria felt a surge of nervous energy. This was it - their chance to uncover the truth and possibly change everything.

"Okay," David said, pulling up a detailed schematic of the Emotional Regulation Center. "Let's break this down step by step. Aria, you're going to have to come in through the main entrance. Your old credentials should still work, but we'll need a solid cover story."

Zara nodded, her fingers flying over a keyboard. "I can create a fake mission. Something about a surprise inspection of the new emotional screening protocols. It'll give you an excuse to pry around."

"Good thinking," Evan agreed. "But what about once she's inside? The research wing will be heavily guarded."

Aria leaned forward and studied the layout. "There's a service corridor here," she said, pointing to a narrow passageway on the map. "It's rarely used. If I can get to it, I should be able to bypass most of the security checkpoints."

Tom spoke up, his voice hesitant but determined. "What if you need a diversion? I could turn myself in, create a ruckus at the front desk. It might draw some of the guards away from the research wing."

"No way," Aria and Evan said in unison. Aria continued, her voice softening, "Tom, I appreciate the offer, but it's too risky. We're not sacrificing anyone."

David nodded in agreement. "Aria's right. We'll find another way to create a diversion if necessary." He returned to the schematics. "Once you're in the lab, you'll need to work quickly. Download everything you can that has to do with the early days of the Initiative and your mother's research."

"And keep an eye out for anything out of the ordinary," Evan added. "Personal notes, prototypes, anything that might give us insight into what your mother was really thinking."

Aria nodded, trying to calm the butterflies in her stomach. "How long do I have?"

Zara frowned and did some calculations. "Based on their security protocols, we should be able to give you a fifteen minute window when their systems recycle. After that, the risk of detection skyrockets."

"Fifteen minutes," Aria repeated, the enormity of the task sinking in. "That's not much time."

Evan put a reassuring hand on her shoulder. "It's all we need. You can do this, Aria."

She looked up at him, drawing strength from the confidence in his eyes. "Okay. When do we do this?"

David studied the data scrolling across the screen. "The next security cycle that meets our needs is in two days. That gives us time to prepare and for Zara to create your cover identity."

As they continued to refine the plan, discussing contingencies and escape routes, Aria felt a mix of emotions swirl within her. Fear, of course - this was by far the most dangerous thing they'd ever attempted. But also excitement, determination, and a burning curiosity about what she might find in her mother's old lab.

Hours passed in a frenzy of preparation. They went over the plan again and again, refining each step until it was seared into Aria's memory. When they finally broke to rest, the first hints of dawn peeked through the warehouse windows.

As the others drifted off to sleep, Aria once again found herself drawn to the window overlooking the city. The Emotional Regulation Center loomed in the distance, no longer a symbol of oppression, but now a treasure trove of potential answers.

She felt Evan's presence before he spoke, a comforting warmth at her back. "You should get some sleep," he said quietly. "Big day ahead."

Aria turned to face him, drinking in the sight of his concerned eyes and gentle smile. "I know. I just... I can't stop thinking about it. About her."

Evan nodded in understanding. "Your mother."

"Yes," Aria sighed. "I keep trying to reconcile the woman I knew - cold, logical, devoted to the Initiative - with the idea that she might have had doubts. That she might have tried to change things."

Evan took her hand, his thumb tracing soothing circles on her palm. "People are complex, Aria. Even in a world that tries to strip away that complexity. Your mother may have been both - the architect of the Initiative and someone who saw its flaws."

Aria leaned into him, drawing comfort from his steady presence. "I'm scared, Evan," she admitted in a whisper. "Not just of getting caught, but... what if what we find changes everything I thought I knew about her? About myself?"

Evan wrapped his arms around her, pulling her close. "Whatever we find, we'll face it together. You're not alone in this, Aria. Not anymore."

As they stood there, the city slowly coming to life beyond the window, Aria felt a sense of calm settle over her. Yes, the task ahead was daunting. Yes, the answers they might find could shake the foundations of everything she'd believed. But here, in Evan's arms, with the support of her newfound family behind her, she felt ready to face whatever came next.

In two days, she would step back into her old life, don the mask of a Collector once more. But this time, it would be different. This time, she would be fighting for the truth, for freedom, for a future where everyone could feel the full spectrum of human emotion.

As sleep finally began to tug at her consciousness, Aria made a silent promise to herself and to the mother she barely knew. She would uncover the truth, no matter the cost. And somehow, someway, she would make things right.

The die was cast. In two days, everything would change. Aria only hoped they were ready for whatever lay ahead.

TWELVE

INTO THE LION'S DEN

Aria's heart pounded as she adjusted the collar of her old Collector uniform. The fabric felt strange against her skin now, a reminder of the life she'd left behind. She caught her reflection in a broken piece of mirror and barely recognized herself. Her eyes, once cold and distant, now burned with a mixture of determination and fear.

"You don't have to do this," Evan said quietly, coming up behind her. His reflection joined hers in the mirror, concern etched into his face.

Aria turned to him, squaring her shoulders. "Yes, I do. We need answers and this is our best chance to get them."

Evan nodded, his expression a mixture of pride and concern. He reached out and adjusted her badge slightly. "Just... be careful in there. If anything feels off..."

"I'm aborting the mission immediately," Aria finished. "I know, Evan. We've been over this plan a hundred times."

He smiled ruefully. "Can you blame me for being concerned?"

Aria's expression softened. She leaned in and planted a soft kiss on his lips. "I'll be careful. I promise."

A throat cleared behind them. They turned to see Zara, her usual grin tempered by the gravity of the situation. "Hate to break up the love fest, but it's time."

They gathered around the makeshift command center one last time. David's fingers flew over the keyboard, bringing up a detailed map of the Emotional Regulation Center.

"Remember," he said, his voice tense, "you have a fifteen minute window when the security systems recycle. Get in, find what you can in your mother's old lab, and get out. Not a second more."

Aria nodded, memorizing the route. "And if I get stopped?"

"You're there for a surprise inspection," Tom supplied. "Collecting data on the new emotional screening protocols."

"Right," Aria took a deep breath, steeling herself. "Okay. I'm ready."

The ride to the center was a blur of tension and carefully rehearsed movements. Aria kept her face impassive, channeling the emotionless demeanor she'd worn for so many years. Inside, however, her mind raced and her heart thundered.

As she approached the main entrance, a familiar voice called out. "Collector Thorne?"

Aria turned and came face to face with Maya. Her former colleague's eyes widened in surprise.

"Maya," Aria said, keeping her voice level through sheer force of will. "I didn't expect to see you here."

Maya's brow furrowed in confusion. "We thought... There were reports that you were..."

"Undercover," Aria cut in smoothly, thanking whatever luck had made her remember her cover story. "A classified operation. I'm here to report my findings."

For a moment, Maya looked skeptical. Then she nodded slowly. "Of course. My apologies, Collector Thorne. Shall I escort you to the briefing room?"

Aria's mind raced. This wasn't part of the plan, but refusing might arouse suspicion. "Actually," she said, thinking quickly, "I need to retrieve some data from the old research wing first. You know, classified information and all that."

Maya hesitated, then nodded. "Of course. Do you need any help?"

"No," Aria said, perhaps too quickly. She forced a smile. "But thank you, Maya. I'll find my way."

As she walked away, Aria could feel Maya's eyes boring into her back. Fighting the urge to run, she kept her measured pace until she rounded a corner and was out of sight.

"That was too close," Zara's voice crackled in her earpiece. "Are you okay?"

Aria let out a shaky breath. "Fine. But we have to hurry. Maya might start asking questions."

She made her way through the familiar corridors, each step bringing back memories of her life as a Collector. It felt like a lifetime ago.

Finally, she reached the door to her mother's old laboratory. Her hand shook as she placed it on the biometric scanner. For a heart-stopping moment, nothing happened. Then, with a soft beep, the door slid open.

"I'm in," she whispered into her comm.

"Clock's ticking," David's tense voice replied. "Fourteen minutes."

Aria stepped into the lab, memories washing over her. The stark white walls, the humming equipment, the lingering scent of antiseptic - it was all just as she remembered it.

She moved quickly to the main computer terminal and inserted the drive Zara had given her. As the files began to download, she scanned the room, looking for anything that might hold answers.

Her eyes fell on a small safe tucked away in a corner. Heart pounding, she approached it. The combination... what would her mother have used?

On impulse, she entered her own date of birth. The safe clicked open.

Inside was a single data chip and a handwritten note. With trembling fingers, Aria unfolded the paper.

Aria,

If you're reading this, I hope it means you've woken up to the truth. What I've done is unforgivable, but perhaps with this information you can make it right. I'm so sorry, my love. For everything.

Love, Mom

Tears stung Aria's eyes as she put the note and chip in her pocket.

"Aria," Evan's urgent voice came over the comm. "We have a problem. Maya's headed your way with security."

Panic surged through her. "The download?"

"Ninety percent," Zara replied. "Just a few more seconds."

Aria's mind raced. She could hear footsteps approaching. The download ended with a soft chime and she yanked the drive free.

Just as she was about to run, her eyes fell on a small vial labeled "Emotional Catalyst". Without thinking, she grabbed it and shoved it into her bag.

The door slid open just as Aria sat up. Maya stood there, flanked by two Enforcers, her expression a mixture of betrayal and determination.

"Collector Thorne," Maya said, her voice cold. "You are under arrest for emotional deviance and treason against the state."

Aria's heart sank. She was trapped, with no way out and the weight of vital information literally in her pockets.

As the Enforcers approached, Aria made a split-second decision. She pulled the vial from her pocket and smashed it on the ground between them.

A cloud of shimmering particles filled the air. Maya and the Enforcers stumbled back, coughing and disoriented.

Aria held her breath and ran, pushing past them into the hallway. Alarms blared as she sprinted through the building, her lungs burning and her vision blurred with unshed tears.

She burst out of an emergency exit, gasping for the cool night air. A nondescript van screeched to a halt beside her, its side door sliding open to reveal Evan's worried face.

"Go, go, go!" Aria yelled as she jumped into the van.

As they sped away from the center, Aria finally allowed herself to breathe. She'd done it. She had the information. But at what cost?

The van was silent, except for the sound of labored breathing and the distant wail of sirens. Aria looked at her friends' faces - worried, relieved, questioning - and knew that nothing would ever be the same again.

Whatever was on that data chip and in those downloaded files had better be worth it. For there was no turning back now. The real battle was about to begin.

THIRTEEN
REVELATIONS

Aria's hands shook as she held the data chip, her mother's last message burning a hole in her pocket. The van sped through the night, putting distance between them and the Emotional Regulation Center, but she couldn't shake the feeling that they were still being watched, hunted.

"Aria?" Evan's voice was soft, tinged with concern. "Are you okay?"

She looked up and met his worried gaze. The adrenaline was wearing off, leaving her feeling hollow and shaky. "I... I don't know," she admitted, her voice barely above a whisper.

Zara turned from the front seat, her usual bravado subdued. "What happened in there? We lost contact for a few minutes and then all hell broke loose."

Aria took a deep breath and tried to organize her thoughts. "I found my mother's old lab. There was a safe... inside it was this chip and a note." She pulled out the folded paper, smoothing it with trembling fingers.

"What does it say?" David asked from the driver's seat, his eyes flicking to the rearview mirror.

Aria read the note aloud, her voice caught in the words. When she finished, a heavy silence fell over the van.

"She knew," Tom said quietly, breaking the silence. "She knew it was wrong."

Evan's arm tightened around Aria's shoulders. "What's on the chip?"

"I don't know," Aria replied, turning the small device over in her hands. "But whatever it is, my mother thought it was important enough to hide."

"We have to be careful how we access it," David warned. "It could be encrypted, or worse, tagged for tracking."

Zara nodded, already pulling out a specialized tablet. "I can set up a secure, isolated system to read it. It'll take some time, but it's safer than just plugging it in."

As Zara went to work, Aria leaned into Evan's embrace, the events of the night catching up with her. "I saw Maya," she said quietly, guilt gnawing at her. "She... she tried to stop me. I used this vial I found, some kind of emotional catalyst. I don't know what it did to her."

Evan's hand made soothing circles on her back. "You did what you had to do. Maya made her choice when she sided with the Enforcers."

Aria nodded, but the knot in her stomach didn't loosen. She closed her eyes and saw again the look of betrayal on Maya's face, the confusion as the contents of the vial filled the air.

"Guys," Zara's excited voice cut through Aria's thoughts. "I've got something. The contents of the chip are decoding."

They all leaned forward as Zara's tablet came to life, lines of text and diagrams filling the screen.

"Oh my God," David breathed, his eyes widening as he scanned the information. "This is... this changes everything."

Aria's heart raced. "What is it? What did my mother find?"

David looked up, his face a mixture of awe and horror. "The Initiative... it wasn't just about suppressing emotions. It was designed to redirect them, to channel them into specific individuals."

"Like Aria," Evan said, the pieces falling into place.

David nodded grimly. "Exactly. But that's not all. The repression wasn't supposed to be permanent. There was supposed to be a reversal process, a way to gradually reintroduce emotions into the population."

Aria felt as if the floor had been pulled out from under her. "But... why? Why do all this just to undo it?"

"Control," Zara said, her voice hard. "Imagine if you had the power to give or take away people's ability to feel. You could shape entire societies, manipulate people on a massive scale."

The implications were staggering. Aria's mind reeled, trying to process the enormity of what they'd discovered.

"There's more," David continued, scrolling through the data. "Your mother was working on a way to reverse the process en masse. Some kind of emotional antidote that could be dispersed through the air filtration systems."

"The vial," Aria gasped, remembering the small container she'd smashed during her escape. "The emotional catalyst. Could that have been it?"

David's brow furrowed. "Possibly. But without knowing the exact formula, there's no way to be sure of its effects or safety."

A tense silence fell over the group as they absorbed the weight of this new information.

"So what do we do now?" Tom asked, his voice small but firm.

Evan straightened, fire in his eyes. "We finish what Aria's mother started. We find a way to reverse the Initiative, to give people their emotions back."

"It won't be that easy," David warned. "The Council won't just stand by and let us undo everything they've built."

"No," Aria said, a newfound determination strengthening her voice. "But we have to try. For everyone who's lived half a life, for everyone who's been used as an emotional battery. We have to make it right."

She looked around at her friends' faces and saw the determination reflected in them. They were tired, scared, and now burdened with knowledge that could change the world. But they were together.

"First things first," Zara said, always practical. "We need a safe place to analyze all this data and start working on a plan."

David nodded. "I know a place. An old research facility outside the city limits. It's off the grid, should be safe for us to regroup and strategize."

As the van changed course and headed for this new sanctuary, Aria felt a mix of emotions swirl within her. Fear, certainly - they were now bigger targets than ever. But also hope, determination, and a fierce love for the people around her who had become her family.

She looked down at the note from her mother, tracing the words with her finger. "I'm going to make this right," she whispered, a promise to herself and to the woman who had set all of this in motion. "Somehow, I'm going to fix this."

Evan's hand found hers and squeezed gently. No words were needed; his touch said it all. Whatever came next, they would face it together.

As the city lights faded behind them, Aria allowed herself a moment of quiet reflection. They had answers now, but those answers had only led to bigger questions, bigger challenges. The real battle was just beginning.

But for the first time since it all began, Aria felt truly ready. Ready to face the truth about her past, ready to fight for a future where everyone could feel the full spectrum of human emotion.

The road ahead was uncertain, fraught with danger. But with her newfound family by her side and the fire of purpose burning within her, Aria knew one thing for certain:

She would change the world.

FOURTEEN
ECHOES AND RIPPLES

The old research facility loomed before them, a hulking silhouette against the pre-dawn sky. Aria stared up at it, a chill running down her spine that had nothing to do with the cool morning air.

"Are you sure this place is safe?" Zara asked, voicing the concern they all felt.

David nodded, his eyes scanning the area. "As safe as it can be right now. It's been abandoned for years, off all official records."

They made their way inside, the musty air and layers of dust a testament to the building's long disuse. But as David flipped a switch and old generators hummed to life, Aria felt a spark of hope. This could work. This could be their base of operations.

As the others set about making the room habitable, Aria found herself drawn to a large window overlooking the distant city skyline. The Emotional Regulation Center was just visible on the horizon, a looming reminder of every-thing they were fighting against.

"Hey," Evan's voice was soft as he joined her. "How are you holding up?"

Aria turned to him, drinking in the warmth and concern in his eyes. "I'm... processing," she admitted. "It's all so much. My mother, the truth about the Initiative... I feel like everything I thought I knew has been turned upside down."

Evan's hand found hers, his touch grounding her. "I know. But Aria, you're not alone. We're all here, and we'll figure it out together."

She nodded, squeezing his hand in silent thanks. Over his shoulder, she could see the others hard at work. Zara was setting up a makeshift command center, her fingers flying over keyboards as she established secure lines of communication. Tom and David pored over the schematics they'd stolen, trying to make sense of the complex formulas and diagrams.

"We should help," Aria said, snapping out of her reverie.

They joined the others, and soon the room was a hive of activity. Hours passed in a blur of data analysis, strategy discussions, and attempts to synthesize the vast amount of information they'd uncovered.

As the sun began to set, casting long shadows across the room, David called for a break. "We need to rest, regroup," he said, his voice tired but determined. "We're no good to anyone if we burn ourselves out."

They gathered around a makeshift table, sharing a meager meal of canned goods and stale crackers. The mood was somber, the weight of their discoveries hanging heavily in the air.

"So," Tom said, breaking the silence. "What's our next move?"

All eyes turned to Aria. She swallowed hard, feeling the weight of their expectations. "We need to find a way to mass produce the emotional catalyst," she said slowly. "My mother's notes suggest it could be the key to reversing the effects of the Initiative."

Zara nodded, her brow furrowed in thought. "But we'd need access to a proper laboratory, specialized equipment. Not to mention the raw materials."

"And a way to distribute it," Evan added. "Even if we could make it, how would we get it to the entire population?"

The questions hung in the air, each one a daunting obstacle. Aria felt a wave of despair threaten to overwhelm her. How could they hope to succeed against such odds?

But then she looked around at the faces of her friends - tired, yes, but still determined, still fighting. And she felt a surge of determination.

"We'll start small," she said, her voice rising with each word. "We find a way to produce a limited amount of the catalyst. Then we target key individuals - people in positions of influence who might be sympathetic to our cause."

David's eyes brightened with understanding. "If we can awaken even a few people in the right places, it could create a ripple effect."

"Exactly," Aria nodded, warming to the idea. "We create pockets of awakened individuals, build a network. And all the while, we work to find a way to spread the catalyst on a larger scale."

The energy in the room shifted, hope sparking in weary eyes.

"It's risky," Evan said, but there was a note of excitement in his voice. "The Council will be on high alert after what happened at the Center."

"Then we have to be smarter," Zara said, a familiar gleam of mischief in her eyes. "More creative in how we operate."

As they began to work out the details of their plan, Aria felt a warmth blossom in her chest. This was what she'd missed all these years as a Collector - purpose, connection, the thrill of fighting for something bigger than herself.

Hours passed as they strategized, the room buzzing with ideas and possibilities. It was well past midnight when David finally called for rest.

As the others settled in for the night, Aria once again found herself drawn to the window. The city glittered in the distance, millions of lives unaware of the truth, of the potential for change that lay within reach.

She felt Evan's presence before he spoke, a comforting warmth at her back. "What are you thinking?" he asked quietly.

Aria turned to face him, struck again by the depth of emotion in his eyes. "Thinking about all the people out there," she said. "About how their lives might change if we succeed. It's... overwhelming."

Evan nodded, understanding in his eyes. "It is. But, Aria, what we're doing-it's important. It's necessary."

"I know," she said, leaning into him. "I'm just... I'm scared, Evan. What if we fail? What if we make things worse?"

He wrapped his arms around her, holding her close. "We might fail," he admitted. "But we have to try. And whatever happens, we face it together."

Aria nodded against his chest, drawing strength from his presence. As they stood there, the first hints of dawn began to lighten the sky.

A new day. A new chance to fight, to make a difference.

Aria took a deep breath, steeling herself for the challenges ahead. They had a long road ahead of them, filled with danger and uncertainty. But they also had hope, determination, and each other.

As the sun rose, casting its warm light over the awakening city, Aria made a silent vow. She would see this through, no matter what the cost. For her mother, for her friends, for every person out there living half a life.

They would bring emotion back to the world. And in doing so, they might just save the soul of humanity.

The battle was far from over. But Aria was ready.

Let the new day begin.

FIFTEEN
FIRST STEPS

Aria's fingers hovered over the vial, her heart pounding in her chest. The pale blue liquid inside seemed to shimmer, almost alive. This was it - her first batch of the emotional catalyst, synthesized from her mother's formula.

"Are you sure?" Evan asked, his voice deep and tense beside her.

Aria met his gaze and saw her own mixture of fear and determination reflected back at her. "No," she admitted. "But we have to start somewhere."

They were in a small, makeshift lab they'd cobbled together in the abandoned research facility. It had taken weeks of careful planning, covert supply runs, and endless hours of work to get to this point. Now it had all come down to this moment.

Zara's voice crackled over the comm system. "The perimeter is clear. But make it quick - we can't risk staying in one place too long."

Aria took a deep breath and steeled herself. Her plan was to test the catalyst on a willing volunteer-someone already sympathetic to their cause, but still under the influence of the Initiative's emotional suppression.

As if on cue, there was a soft knock at the door. David entered, leading a nervous-looking woman in her mid-thirties.

"Aria, Evan, this is Dr. Chen," David introduced. "She's been secretly questioning the Initiative for years."

Dr. Chen managed a small nod, her eyes darting around the room. "I... I'm not sure what to expect," she said, her voice barely above a whisper.

Aria stepped forward and offered what she hoped was a reassuring smile. "It's okay to be nervous. We'll take it slow and you can stop at any time."

As Aria prepared the catalyst for administration, she could feel the weight of everyone's eyes on her. The pressure was immense - if this didn't work, or worse, if it harmed Dr. Chen, their entire mission could be over before it even began.

"Ready?" Aria asked, holding up the prepared injector.

Dr. Chen swallowed hard, then nodded. "Ready."

Aria pressed the injector against Dr. Chen's arm, and with a soft hiss, the catalyst was delivered. For a moment, nothing happened. The room held its collective breath.

Then Dr. Chen gasped, her eyes widening. She stumbled, and Evan moved quickly to support her.

"Dr. Chen?" Aria asked, her voice strained with concern. "How are you feeling?"

The woman blinked quickly, her breathing uneven. "I... I..." She looked up, and Aria was stunned to see tears forming in her eyes. "I feel... everything."

A wave of relief washed over Aria, so strong it made her knees weak. It had worked. They had actually done it.

The next hour was a whirlwind of monitoring Dr. Chen's vitals, asking her questions, and documenting every detail of her awakening. Through it all, the woman alternated between laughing and crying, overwhelmed by the rush of long-suppressed emotions.

When things finally began to calm down, Aria found a quiet moment to slip away. She made her way to the room's small window and looked out at the city sprawling in the distance.

She felt Evan's presence before he spoke, a warm comfort at her back. "You did it," he said softly, pride in his voice.

Aria leaned back against him, allowing herself a moment of vulnerability. "We did it," she corrected. "But Evan, this is only the beginning. One person. How are we ever going to scale this up to the entire population?"

Evan's arms wrapped around her, firm and reassuring. "One step at a time," he murmured. "We've proven it works. That's huge."

She nodded, trying to hold onto that sense of accomplishment. But doubt nagged at her. "And what about the long-term effects? We have no idea how Dr. Chen will handle this in the days and weeks to come."

"That's why we'll continue to monitor her," Evan reminded her. "We'll learn, we'll adjust. That's all we can do."

Their moment was interrupted by Zara's urgent voice over

the comm. "Guys, we've got company. Enforcer patrols moving into the sector."

Aria's heart jumped into her throat. "How close?"

"Too close for comfort," Zara replied grimly. "We need to move. Now."

The next few minutes were a blur of activity. Equipment was hastily packed, data backed up, all traces of their presence erased as best they could.

As they prepared to leave, Dr. Chen caught Aria's arm. "Thank you," she said, her voice thick with emotion. "I know we have to separate for safety, but... thank you for giving me this gift."

Aria felt a lump form in her throat. "Use it wisely," she said. "And stay safe."

They split up, taking different routes out of the facility. As Aria and Evan made their way through back alleys and abandoned buildings, the sound of Enforcer drones buzzed ominously overhead.

"They're getting closer," Evan muttered, pulling Aria into a shadowy doorway as a patrol passed nearby.

Aria's mind raced. Had they been detected? Was there a leak somewhere in their network? Or was this just an unfortunate coincidence?

As they crouched in the darkness, their hearts pounding, Aria felt a strange mixture of fear and exhilaration. They had done it - they had successfully awakened someone. But at what cost? And where would they go from here?

The patrol passed, and they continued their tense journey back to their current safe house. But Aria knew that things had changed irrevocably. They had taken their first real step in the fight against the Initiative.

The question now was: what would be the consequences of that step? And were they really ready for what came next?

As the safe house came into view, Aria squeezed Evan's hand. Whatever challenges lay ahead, they would face them together. They had to. The fate of countless emotionally repressed people now rested on their shoulders.

The real battle was about to begin.

SIXTEEN

RIPPLES AND WAVES

A week had passed since Dr. Chen's awakening, and Aria felt as if she hadn't slept a moment of it. She stared at the array of screens in front of her, each displaying different news feeds and data streams. They had monitored every channel, every whisper, looking for any sign that their actions had been noticed.

"Anything?" Zara asked, pushing a cup of what could charitably be called coffee across the table.

Aria shook her head and rubbed her tired eyes. "Nothing definitive. There's been an increase in reports of 'emotional disturbance' in Dr. Chen's sector, but nothing directly related to her."

Zara frowned and leaned forward to study the screens. "That could be good or bad. Either we've managed to stay under the radar, or..."

"Or they're onto us and just haven't made a move yet," Aria finished grimly.

The door opened and Evan entered, his face drawn with exhaustion. "David made contact with Dr. Chen," he reported. "She's... struggling. The emotional overload is intense, but she's pulling through. Says she wouldn't go back to being repressed for anything."

A mix of relief and concern churned in Aria's stomach. They had given Dr. Chen her emotions back, yes, but at what cost? Were they really helping, or were they just trading one form of suffering for another?

"We need to refine the formula," Aria said, voicing the thought that had been nagging at her for days. "Find a way to ease the transition, make it less overwhelming."

Evan nodded and pulled up a chair next to her. "Agreed. But that's going to take time and resources we don't have."

"Um, guys?" Tom's nervous voice came from the doorway. "You might want to take a look at this."

They gathered around the main screen as Tom pulled up a live news feed. Aria's breath caught in her throat as she recognized the figure addressing the cameras.

"Maya," she whispered.

Her former colleague stood at a podium, her face as impassive as ever. But there was something in her eyes, an intensity that hadn't been there before.

"Citizens," Maya began, her voice clear and authoritative. "The Council has become aware of a dangerous faction attempting to undermine the peace and stability we have all worked so hard to achieve. These individuals, led by former Collector Aria Thorne, are attempting to disrupt our emotional balance and plunge us back into the chaos of unchecked emotion."

Aria felt as if the ground had been pulled out from under her. They knew. Somehow, they knew.

Maya continued, her eyes seeming to bore directly into the camera. "We urge all citizens to remain vigilant. Report any signs of emotional instability or aberration. Remember, emotion is chaos. Order is peace."

The feed cut out, leaving a stunned silence in its wake.

"Well," Zara said, her voice taut, "I guess that answers the question of whether they're on to us."

Aria's mind raced. "We have to warn Dr. Chen, get her to safety before they track her down."

"Already on it," David said, his fingers flying over a keyboard. "But, Aria, this changes everything. We're not just fugitives anymore. We're public enemies."

The weight of it all threatened to crush her. Aria closed her eyes and tried to center herself. When she opened them, she found everyone looking at her, waiting for direction.

"We knew this could happen," she said, surprised at the steadiness in her voice. "It doesn't change our mission. If anything, it makes it more urgent. We need to wake up more people, build our network before the Council can shut us down completely."

Evan's hand found hers and squeezed gently. "It's risky. We'll be fighting a war on two fronts - trying to awaken people while avoiding capture."

"Then we get creative," Zara chimed in, a familiar gleam of determination in her eyes. "Hit-and-run tactics. Guerrilla awakenings. We use their own systems against them."

As they began to brainstorm new strategies, Aria felt a strange calm settle over her. Yes, the situation was dire. Yes, the odds were against them. But looking at her friends' faces-tired but determined, scared but resolute-she knew they had a fighting chance.

Hours passed in a frenzy of planning and preparation. They reached out to their limited network of sympathizers, warning them to hunker down. New safe houses were set up, communication protocols tightened. Through it all, Aria felt like she was walking a tightrope, balancing between hope and despair.

As the others finally succumbed to exhaustion and grabbed what sleep they could, Aria found herself drawn to the window again. The city stretched out before her, millions of lives unaware of the war being waged for their emotional freedom.

"You should rest," Evan's voice came softly from behind her.

Aria turned and offered him a pale smile. "So should you."

He moved to stand beside her, their shoulders touching. For a long moment they just stood in silence, taking comfort in each other's presence.

"Are we doing the right thing?" Aria finally asked, voicing the doubt that had been gnawing at her. "Unleashing all these emotions on people who aren't ready for it?"

Evan was silent for a moment, thinking. "I think," he said slowly, "that living half a life, never really feeling, is worse than any pain emotions could bring. We give people a choice, Aria. The chance to be fully human."

She nodded, letting his words sink in. "I just hope we're strong enough to go through with it. To face whatever comes next."

Evan's arm slipped around her waist, pulling her close. "We are," he said with quiet conviction. "Together we are."

As the first light of dawn began to color the sky, Aria felt a renewed sense of purpose. Yes, the Council knew about her now. Yes, the dangers had grown exponentially. But so had the stakes.

They were no longer a small group of rebels. They were the spark of a revolution, the hope for a world where people could feel, love, grieve, and rejoice without restraint.

Whatever challenges lay ahead, whatever sacrifices they might have to make, Aria knew one thing for certain: they would face it all together. And in that togetherness, in the bonds forged through shared struggle and hope, lay their true strength.

A new day was dawning, bringing with it unknown dangers and possibilities. But as Aria stood there, with Evan at her side and the warmth of purpose in her heart, she felt ready to face it all.

The real battle was about to begin. And they would meet it head on, with every emotion they had reclaimed.

SEVENTEEN
SHADOWS CLOSING IN

Aria's breath came in short, sharp gasps as she ran, her feet pounding the pavement. The alley seemed endless, shadows reaching out like grasping fingers. Behind her, she could hear the rhythmic thud of Enforcer boots and the high-pitched whine of pursuit drones.

"Left!" Zara's voice crackled in her earpiece. "There's a maintenance tunnel on your left!"

Aria turned sharply, almost losing her footing. She spotted the rusty grate and threw herself at it, fingers clutching for hold. For a heart-stopping moment, it refused to budge. Then, with a groan of protesting metal, it swung open.

She tumbled through, pulling the grate behind her as a search beam swept over her former position. Pressed against the damp tunnel wall, Aria held her breath as the Enforcers thundered past her hiding place.

"Aria?" Evan's voice, tight with concern. "Aria, can you hear me?"

"I'm here," she whispered, her voice shaking. "I'm okay. Mission accomplished."

She felt the small vial in her pocket, containing the precious emotional catalyst. Another successful awakening, another life changed forever. But at what cost?

The journey back to the safe house was a blur of back alleys and secret passageways. By the time Aria stumbled through the hidden entrance, she was exhausted, every muscle screaming in protest.

Evan was there in an instant, pulling her into a fierce hug. "I thought we'd lost you," he murmured into her hair.

Aria allowed herself a moment to sink into his warmth before pulling away. "It was close," she admitted. "Too close. They're getting better at anticipating our moves."

The others gathered around, their faces etched with concern and relief. David took the vial from Aria and examined it carefully. "At least we got what we came for. This should be enough to wake up three, maybe four people."

Zara snorted, a bitter note in her voice. "Great. Four more awakened while the Council tightens its grip on millions. We're losing this war."

A heavy silence fell over the room. Aria felt the weight of their expectations, their fears, pressing down on her. She was their leader, the face of the Resistance. She was supposed to have answers.

But in this moment, all she had was doubt.

"Maybe..." Tom's hesitant voice broke the silence. "Maybe we need to think bigger. Go public with what we know."

Evan shook his head. "Too risky. The Council controls all the media channels. They'd shut us down before we could reach anyone."

"Not if we hijack their own systems," Zara said, a spark of her old fire returning. "I've been working on a way to break into their emergency broadcast network. If we could get our message out, even for a few minutes..."

Aria's mind raced through the possibilities. It was audacious, incredibly dangerous... and it might be their only chance to turn the tide.

"What would we even say?" David asked, voicing the question on everyone's mind. "How do you convince an entire population that everything they've ever known is a lie?"

Aria closed her eyes, remembering her own awakening. The confusion, the fear, the overwhelming rush of emotions. And then... clarity. Purpose. Life in full color.

"We tell them the truth," she said, her voice growing stronger with each word. "About the Initiative, about what was done to them. We show them what they've missed."

Evan's hand found hers and squeezed gently. "It's a big risk," he said quietly. "If it backfires, we lose any chance of staying under the radar."

Aria met his gaze and saw her own mixture of fear and determination reflected back at her. "I know. But we're running out of options. And out of time."

The room fell silent again as the weight of the decision settled over them. This wasn't just another mission. This was a turning point, a moment that could change everything.

Finally, David spoke. "If we're going to do this, we need to be smart about it. We're going to need a safe place to broadcast from, a foolproof plan to break into their systems, and a message that will cut through years of conditioning."

Zara nodded, already pulling up schematics on her tablet. "I can handle the technical side. Give me a week, maybe two, and I can get us into their network."

"I can work on the embassy," Tom offered. "I... I remember what it was like to wake up. Maybe I can find a way to explain it that will resonate with people."

One by one, they all chimed in, offering ideas and support. Aria felt a surge of emotion as she looked at her team - her family. They were tired, scared, pushed to their limits. But they were still fighting, still believing in the possibility of a better world.

As the others began to plan in earnest, Aria slipped away, needing a moment to breathe. She found herself in the small room that served as her quarters, sinking onto the narrow bed.

A soft knock on the door. "Aria?" Evan's voice, soft and concerned. "Can I come in?"

"Yes," she called, managing a small smile as he entered.

He sat down next to her, close enough that she could feel the warmth of his body. For a long moment, neither spoke.

"Are we doing the right thing?" Aria finally asked, voicing the doubt that had been gnawing at her. "Going forward with this plan? We could be putting everyone in danger."

Evan was silent for a moment, thinking. "I think," he said slowly, "that sometimes the right thing and the safe thing aren't the same thing. We're fighting for people's right to feel, to really live. That's worth the risk."

Aria nodded, letting his words sink in. She leaned into him, drawing strength from his presence. "I'm afraid, Evan," she admitted in a whisper. "Not just of failing, but of succeeding. What if we win and the world isn't ready for what comes next?"

Evan's arm slipped around her waist, pulling her close. "Then we'll face that together, too. One step at a time, remember?"

As they sat there, the sounds of the others' planning filtering through the thin walls, Aria felt a complicated mix of emotions swirling within her. Fear, yes, and uncertainty. But also hope, determination, and a fierce love for the people who had become her family.

Whatever came next, whatever challenges they faced, they would face them head on. Together.

The battle for humanity's emotional freedom was about to enter a new phase. And Aria was ready to lead the charge.

EIGHTEEN
THE MESSAGE

The abandoned station loomed before them, a hulking silhouette against the pre-dawn sky. Aria's heart raced as she scanned the area, looking for any sign of Enforcer activity.

"Zara?" she whispered into her comm. "We clear?"

"As clear as we're going to get," Zara's tense voice crackled back. "The security systems are looped. You've got a ten-minute window. Make it count."

Aria nodded to Evan and Tom, and they moved quickly across the open floor. The station door yielded to Zara's hacked access code, and they slipped inside.

The interior was a maze of dusty equipment and tangled wires. Aria's eyes strained in the dim emergency lighting as they made their way to the main control room.

"Here," Tom said, pointing to a bank of antiquated but functional-looking consoles. "This should do it."

As Tom and Zara (remotely connected) worked to set up the broadcast, Aria paced the small room. The weight of what they were about to do pressed down on her, making it hard to breathe.

Evan caught her hand as she passed and pulled her to a stop. "Hey," he said quietly, his eyes searching hers. "You've got this. We've got this."

Aria managed a shaky smile. "I hope you're right. Because if we're not..."

"Two minutes!" Zara's urgent voice cut through the tension. "Get ready!"

Aria stepped in front of the antique camera, her heart pounding so hard she was sure it would show on the screen. Tom gave her a thumbs up as he made the final adjustments.

"Thirty seconds," Zara counted down. "Twenty... ten... five, four, three, two..."

A red light flashed, and suddenly Aria was live, on every screen in the city.

She took a deep breath and began to speak.

"Citizens of the city, my name is Aria Thorne. You may know me as a fugitive, a danger to society. But I'm here to tell you the truth - a truth that has been hidden from all of us for far too long."

Her voice grew stronger as she continued, passion permeating every word.

"The Emotional Regulation Initiative we've been told keeps us safe and stable is a lie. It doesn't suppress our emotions - it steals them, redirecting them to a select few while leaving the rest of us numb, half-alive."

She held up a vial of the catalyst, the pale blue liquid catching the light.

"This is the key to your freedom. A way to regain the emotions that have been taken from you. I know because I've experienced it myself. I've felt the rush of joy, the pain of sorrow, the fire of anger - all the things that make us truly human."

Aria's voice cracked slightly as she continued, raw emotion bleeding through.

"I know you're scared. I know the idea of feeling again after so long is terrifying. But please, listen to your heart-that small voice inside that's been whispering all along that something is wrong."

She leaned closer to the camera, her eyes intense.

"You don't have to live like this. You don't have to be a cog in a machine, going through the motions of a half-lived life. You can feel again. You can love, grieve, hope, dream. You can be fully, gloriously human."

A warning light began to flash. Her time was almost up.

"The Council will try to silence us, to tell you this is all a lie. But deep down you know the truth. Reach out. Find us. Join us. Together, we can reclaim our humanity and build a world where everyone is free to feel."

The broadcast ended abruptly as the alarm began to sound. They had overstayed their window.

"Move!" Evan yelled, already heading for the exit. "Now!"

They ran, hearts pounding, adrenaline surging. Outside, the whine of approaching drones filled the air.

"This way!" Tom shouted, heading for a hidden access tunnel they'd scouted earlier.

They dove in as searchlights swept over their position. The

tunnel was narrow and damp, forcing them to move single file through the darkness.

After what felt like hours, but was probably only minutes, they emerged into another part of the city. The streets were in chaos, people milling about in confusion, many of them staring at public displays that now showed only static.

"Did it work?" Tom asked between gasps. "Did we reach them?"

Aria looked around, seeing the confusion on people's faces, the first stirrings of questions in their eyes. "I think... I think we did. But now comes the hard part."

They made their way back to the safe house, moving cautiously through the confused crowd. Inside, they found the others gathered around a bank of monitors, each showing a different news feed.

"...dangerous propaganda from known fugitives," a Council spokesman said on one screen. "Citizens are reminded that emotional stability is vital to the well-being of our society."

But on another channel, a reporter looked shaken, her usual composure cracking. "We... we're receiving reports of spontaneous emotional outbursts in several sectors. The Council is urging calm, but... but I..." She trailed off, a look of confusion crossing her face.

Zara muted the feeds and turned to face her. "It's happening," she said, a mixture of awe and fear in her voice. "People are starting to wonder. To feel."

Aria sank into a chair, the enormity of what they had done washing over her. They had lit the spark. Now they had to be ready for the fire that would follow.

"What's our next move?" David asked, his voice calm despite the tension evident in his posture.

Aria looked around at her team - her family. They were tired, scared, but there was a new fire in their eyes. A sense of purpose burning brighter than ever.

"We keep going," she said, her voice firm. "We bring the Catalyst to as many people as we can. We build our network, protect those who awaken. And we prepare."

"Prepare for what?" Tom asked.

Aria's gaze was steely as she answered. "For the fight of our lives. The Council won't take this lying down. They'll come at us with everything they've got. But we'll be ready."

As they began to plan their next steps, Aria felt a complex mix of emotions swirl within her. Fear, yes, and uncertainty about the challenges ahead. But also hope, fierce and bright. They had taken a huge risk, and it was paying off. People were starting to wake up.

The road ahead would be hard, fraught with danger. But looking at her team, feeling the determination that radiated from each of them, Aria knew they could face whatever came next.

The revolution had begun. And they were ready to see it through, no matter the cost.

NINETEEN

UNEXPECTED ALLY

Aria's eyes burned from staring at the screens for hours. Every news feed, every security camera they could hack into - they all told the same story. The city was waking up, and it was chaotic.

"Another riot in Sector 7," Zara reported, her voice strained with exhaustion. "Enforcers are struggling to contain it."

Aria nodded, a mix of emotions swirling in her gut. Pride in what they'd accomplished, fear of what might come next, and a nagging guilt for the chaos they'd unleashed.

"Any word from our contacts?" she asked, turning to David.

The older man shook his head, worry lines deepening on his forehead. "Nothing yet. But that could be good news - means they haven't been caught."

A commotion at the door made them all jump. Evan burst in, breathing heavily, his clothes disheveled.

"Evan!" Aria was on her feet in an instant, her heart in her throat. "What happened? Are you okay?"

He nodded, catching his breath. "I'm fine. But you need to see this."

He pulled out a small data drive and plugged it into her system. A video began to play, and Aria's blood ran cold.

It was Maya, her former colleague, standing at a podium. But this wasn't the cool, professional Maya she remembered. This Maya's eyes burned with an intensity Aria had never seen before.

"Citizens," Maya's voice rang out, clear and passionate. "We have been lied to. The emotional repression we've been living under... it's not for our protection. It's control. I know because I've experienced the truth myself."

Aria's jaw dropped. "She's awake," she whispered. "But how?"

The pieces fell into place in her mind - the vial she'd smashed during her escape from the Emotional Regulation Center. The catalyst must have affected Maya.

Maya continued, her voice rising. "I stand here today in support of Aria Thorne and her message. The Council has betrayed us all. It's time to reclaim our emotions, our humanity."

The video abruptly cut off, replaced by the stern face of a Council member denouncing Maya as a traitor.

Silence fell over the room as they all processed what they had just seen.

"This changes everything," Tom said, voicing what they were all thinking.

Aria's mind raced. Maya's defection was a huge victory for their cause, but it also raised the stakes enormously. The Council would be out for blood now.

"We have to get to her," Aria decided, already heading for the door. "Before the Council does."

Evan grabbed her arm, his eyes filled with concern. "Aria, wait. It could be a trap."

She paused, the logic of his words fighting her instincts. "Maybe. But if it's not... Maya could be a powerful ally. And if it is a trap, better we set it on our terms."

There was a tense silence as the others exchanged glances. Finally, David nodded. "She's right. But we do this smart. Zara, can you trace where the transmission came from?"

Zara's fingers were already flying over the keyboard. "On it. Give me ten minutes."

While the others prepared, Aria felt Evan's presence at her side. "Are you okay?" he asked quietly.

She met his gaze and saw her own mixture of hope and fear reflected back. "I don't know," she admitted. "This is happening so fast. What if we're in over our heads?"

Evan's hand found hers and squeezed gently. "We probably are," he said with a wry smile. "But we're in this together. And, Aria... what we do matters. Look."

He gestured to one of the screens, where footage showed people hugging in the streets, laughing and crying, experiencing real emotion for the first time in years.

"It's because of you," Evan said quietly. "Because you had the courage to tell the truth."

Aria felt a lump form in her throat, overwhelmed by the weight of it all. Before she could respond, Zara's triumphant voice cut through the moment.

"Got it! The transmission came from an old community

center in Sector 4. It's been abandoned for years, but I'm picking up power usage and communication signals."

"All right," Aria said, squaring her shoulders. "Let's go. Zara, you and David stay here and monitor the situation. The rest of us will go check it out."

As they geared up, Aria caught sight of her reflection in a dusty mirror. The woman staring back at her looked different - harder, more determined, but with a fire in her eyes that hadn't been there before. She barely recognized herself.

"Ready?" Evan asked, appearing at her side.

Aria nodded, pushing her doubts aside. "Ready. Let's go find Maya."

As they slipped out into the chaotic streets, Aria's mind whirled with possibilities. If Maya really was on their side now, this could be the turning point they needed. But if it was a trap...

She pushed the thought aside. Whatever came next, they would face it together. The city was changing, awakening to long-suppressed emotions. And Aria was at the center of it all, for better or worse.

The community center loomed ahead, dark and seemingly abandoned. But Aria could feel a tension in the air, a sense that something important was waiting inside.

"Everyone stay alert," she whispered as they approached the entrance. "We don't know what we're walking into."

With a deep breath, Aria pushed open the door and stepped into the unknown. Whatever lay ahead, there was no turning back now. The next chapter of their revolution was about to begin.

TWENTY
BETRAYAL AND CAPTURE

The community center was eerily quiet, dust motes dancing in the dim light filtering through the boarded-up windows. Aria's heart pounded as they moved deeper into the building, every sense on high alert.

"I don't like this," Tom whispered, his eyes darting nervously. "It feels too easy."

Aria nodded, the same thought nagging at her. But before she could answer, a voice came from the shadows.

"I thought you weren't coming."

Maya stepped into view, and Aria's breath caught in her throat. Her former colleague looked... different. Gone was the cool, professional demeanor. This Maya's eyes blazed with intensity, her posture tense with barely contained energy.

"Maya," Aria said cautiously, aware of Evan and Tom flanking her protectively. "Is it really you? Are you... awake?"

A smile broke across Maya's face, transforming her features. "It is. And I am. Aria, I... I owe you an apology. And my thanks."

Aria's guard dropped slightly, hope rising in her chest. "The catalyst... when I smashed the vial..."

Maya nodded eagerly. "It was like waking up from a dream. Suddenly everything was so clear. The lies we'd been told, the life we'd been denied." Her expression darkened. "The damage we'd done as Gatherers."

A lump formed in Aria's throat. She knew the guilt all too well. "Maya, I-"

But Maya cut her off, stepping closer. "No time for this now. Aria, we don't have long. The Council is in chaos, but they're regrouping. They're planning something big, something to quell this awakening before it spreads further."

Aria's mind raced. "What do you mean? What are they planning?"

Maya opened her mouth to answer, but a sudden explosion shook the building. Dust and debris rained down as alarms blared in the distance.

"It's a trap!" Evan yelled, grabbing Aria's arm. "We have to move, now!"

But Maya was already shaking her head, her eyes wide with panic. "No, this isn't... I didn't... They must have followed me!"

Another explosion, closer this time. The sound of boots on pavement, of Enforcer drones whining overhead.

"There's a back way out," Maya said urgently, gesturing for them to follow. "Through the old gym. Hurry!"

They ran, hearts pounding as the sounds of pursuit grew closer. Aria's mind whirled. Had Maya betrayed them? Or had she really not known about the trap?

They burst into the gym, a cavernous space filled with shadows and abandoned equipment. Maya headed for a door on the far side, but came to a halt when it burst open, revealing a squad of Enforcers.

"Aria Thorne," a cold voice rang out, and Aria's blood ran cold. She knew that voice.

Director Kaine stepped into view, his face a mask of cold determination. "I have to admit, you've led us on quite a chase. But it ends here."

Aria's eyes darted around, looking for a way out, but they were surrounded. Enforcers poured in from every entrance, weapons trained on their small group.

"Director," she said, fighting to keep her voice steady. "You don't have to do this. You must see by now that the Initiative is wrong, that we've been lied to."

Kaine's expression didn't change. "What I see is a threat to the peace and stability we've worked so hard to achieve. Your little revolution ends now, Aria."

Maya stepped forward, her voice passionate. "Listen to her, Director! I've felt it myself - the awakening. We've been living half-lives, and for what? So the Council can control us?"

For a moment, something flickered in Kaine's eyes - doubt, perhaps? But it was gone in an instant, replaced by steely determination.

"Enough," he said coldly. "Enforcers, take them into custody. Use of deadly force is authorized if they resist."

Time seemed to slow. Aria saw Evan tensing beside her, ready to fight. Tom looked frightened but determined. And Maya... Maya's face was a mask of fear and determination.

In that moment, Aria made a decision. They couldn't win this battle, not here, not now. But they could live to fight another day.

"Wait!" she shouted, raising her hands. "We will come peacefully. No one has to get hurt."

"Aria, no!" Evan hissed, but she silenced him with a look.

Kaine studied her for a long moment, suspicion warring with triumph on his face. Finally he nodded. "A wise choice, Collector Thorne. Though I'm afraid it's too late for leniency."

As the Enforcers moved in, cuffing her hands behind her back, Aria's mind raced. This wasn't over. Not by a long shot. They had started a revolution, awakened countless people to the truth. Even if they were captured, the movement would continue.

She caught Evan's eye as they were led away, trying to convey everything she couldn't say out loud. His nod was barely perceptible, but it was enough. He understood. They would find a way out of this, together.

As they were marched out of the community center, Aria saw the chaos her broadcast had caused. People in the streets, some crying, some laughing, some looking lost and confused. Enforcers struggled to maintain order, but it was clear they were fighting a losing battle.

A small smile tugged at Aria's lips, despite the gravity of their situation. They had done this. They had awakened the people, given them back their humanity. Whatever came next, this victory could not be undone.

The Enforcer transport loomed ahead, its dark bulk a promise of imprisonment and probably worse. But as Aria was pushed inside, she held her head up. This was just another chapter in her struggle. And it was far from over.

The doors slammed shut, plunging her into darkness. But in that darkness, Aria felt a glimmer of hope. They had allies now, people awakening all over the city. The Council's days were numbered, even if they didn't know it yet.

As the transport rumbled to life, carrying them to an uncertain fate, Aria made a silent vow. This was not the end. It was only the beginning of a new phase in her revolution.

And she would see it through, no matter what the cost.

TWENTY-ONE
BEHIND ENEMY LINES

The cell was cold, sterile, and oppressively quiet. Aria sat on the hard metal bench, her mind racing despite her outward calm. She could feel the weight of the emotional suppression field pressing down on her, trying to dull her senses, her emotions. But she fought it, clinging to the spark of defiance that burned in her chest.

The door slid open with a soft hiss, and Director Kaine stepped inside. His face was an impassive mask, but Aria could see the tension in his shoulders, the tightness around his eyes.

"Comfortable, Collector Thorne?" he asked, his voice dripping with sarcasm.

Aria held his gaze. "You know, I think I preferred the accommodations at our last safe house. The company was better, for one thing."

A flicker of annoyance crossed Kaine's face. "Your attempts at humor are misplaced. Do you have any idea of the chaos you've unleashed?"

"I'd call it freedom, actually," Aria countered, leaning forward. "Tell me, Director, how does it feel to be on the wrong side of history?"

Kaine's composure cracked for a moment, real anger flashing in his eyes. "Wrong side? We brought peace, stability, order to a world tearing itself apart with emotion!"

"You brought a hollow existence," Aria shot back, feeling her own anger rise. "A half-life where people go through the motions without really living."

Kaine paced the small cell, his agitation palpable. "And what you've done is better? The riots, the violence, the complete breakdown of society?"

Aria stood, facing him despite the heaviness in her limbs. "Growing pains. People are feeling again, really feeling, for the first time in years. It's overwhelming, yes, but it's real. It's human."

For a moment, something flickered in Kaine's eyes - doubt, perhaps? But it was gone in an instant, replaced by cold resolve.

"Enough," he said sharply. "I'm not here to debate philosophy. Where is the rest of your party? Where are you making the catalyst?"

Aria smiled thinly. "Come on, Director. You know I'm not going to tell you."

Kaine's lips pressed into a hard line. "We have ways to make you talk, Thorne. Ways that don't require your cooperation."

A shiver ran down Aria's spine, but she held her ground. "Do your worst. I've already won. We've already won. You can't stop what's happening out there."

The Director studied her for a long moment, his expression unreadable. Then, without another word, he turned and left the cell.

As the door closed behind him, Aria sank back onto the bench, her bravado crumbling. She was scared, more scared than she'd ever been. Not for herself, but for Evan, for her friends, for all the people out there waking up to their emotions.

She closed her eyes and tried to center herself. They had known this could happen. They had planned for it. Now she just had to trust her team, the network they had built.

Hours passed in a haze of worry and forced inactivity. The emotional suppression field weighed heavily on her, making it difficult to think, to feel. But Aria clung to her memories, to the fire that had driven her this far.

A commotion in the hallway jolted her from her thoughts. Shouts, the sound of running feet. Then, suddenly, the cell door slid open.

Evan stood there, breathing heavily, a stolen Enforcer uniform hanging loosely from his frame. "Aria," he breathed, relief in his voice. "Are you okay?"

She was on her feet in an instant and threw herself into his arms. "Evan! How did you..."

"No time," he cut her off, already pulling her toward the door. "We've got about two minutes before they realize what's happening."

As they raced through the corridors of the detention center, alarms began to sound. Aria's heart pounded, adrenaline cutting through the fog of the suppression field.

"The others?" she gasped as they ran.

"Safe," Evan assured her. "Zara's hacked the security systems. Tom and David are creating a diversion topside."

They burst out of a service exit into the cool night air. A nondescript van idled nearby, its engine humming quietly.

As they climbed in, Aria caught a glimpse of the city beyond. Fires burned in the distance, and the sound of sirens filled the air. But there was something else - laughter, music, the sounds of life being lived fully and passionately.

"It's working," she murmured, awe in her voice. "It's really working."

Evan squeezed her hand as the van pulled away from the curb. "It is. And we're just getting started."

As they sped through the awakening city, Aria felt a surge of hope, bright and fierce. They had faced capture and come out the other side. The Council's days were numbered, even if they didn't know it yet.

Whatever came next, whatever challenges lay ahead, Aria knew one thing for certain: they would face them together, with every emotion they had regained.

The revolution was far from over. In fact, it was just beginning.

TWENTY-TWO
AWAKENING STORM

The safe house was a hive of activity when Aria and Evan arrived. Zara's fingers flew over keyboards, monitoring the chaos in the city. Tom and David huddled over maps, planning their next move. And in the corner, looking both out of place and right at home, stood Maya.

Aria's former colleague turned unexpected ally rushed forward, relief written all over her face. "Aria! Thank God you're okay. I was so worried when-"

"When your trap failed?" Aria interrupted, unable to keep the edge out of her voice.

Maya flinched as if slapped. "No! Aria, I swear, I had no idea. You must have followed me, or... or tracked me somehow."

Evan stepped between them, his voice deep and calming. "Let's all take a breath. We're all on the same side here, right?"

Aria studied Maya's face, looking for any sign of deception. But all she saw was genuine concern and a depth of emotion that the old Maya had never shown.

"Okay," Aria said finally, some of the tension easing from her shoulders. "Tell me everything. What's going on out there?"

For the next hour, they pored over reports and footage from all over the city. The picture that emerged was one of beautiful chaos. People were awakening in waves, centuries of suppressed emotions bursting like a dam.

"The Council is losing control," Zara reported, a wild grin on her face. "Their ranks of Enforcers are thinning as more of them awaken."

David nodded, his expression a mixture of hope and concern. "But it's not all good news. There's also violence, people who can't handle the intensity of what they're feeling."

Aria felt the weight of responsibility settle on her shoulders. They had started this, and now they had to see it through.

"We have to guide them," she said, her voice strong with newfound purpose. "Show them how to channel these emotions in a positive way."

"And how do we do that?" Tom asked, his eyes wide with a mixture of fear and excitement.

Aria turned to Maya, an idea forming. "We use the Council's own tools against them. Maya, you still have access to the emergency broadcast system, right?"

Maya nodded slowly, understanding dawning on her face. "Yes, but... Aria, are you suggesting what I think you are?"

"A citywide broadcast," Aria confirmed. "Not just a message this time, but a guide. A way to help people understand and accept what they're feeling."

The room erupted in a flurry of planning and preparation. Zara worked to secure her transmission while David and Tom gathered stories and testimonials from awakened individuals.

As the others worked, Evan pulled Aria aside, concern in his eyes. "Are you sure about this? It's a big risk. The Council will do everything they can to stop us."

Aria reached up and gently cupped his face. "I'm sure. Evan, we can't stop now. We owe it to everyone out there to see this through."

He nodded, leaning into her touch. "Okay. Then we'll do it together."

Hours later, they were ready. The makeshift studio they'd set up hummed with nervous energy. Aria sat in front of the camera, her heart pounding but her resolve firm.

"We're live in 3... 2... 1..." Zara counted down, and then they were on.

Aria took a deep breath and began to speak.

"Citizens of the city, this is Aria Thorne. I know many of you are scared, overwhelmed by the emotions you're feeling. But I'm here to tell you that what you're feeling is natural, beautiful, and fundamentally human."

She went on to guide viewers through techniques for processing their emotions, shared stories of others who had awakened, and painted a picture of the living, feeling world they were fighting for.

As she spoke, reports began to pour in. People gathering in the streets, not in riot, but in celebration. Neighbors helping neighbors work through emotional outbursts. The first stirrings of a society relearning how to feel.

But then, halfway through the broadcast, the alarm sounded. Zara's voice cut through the din: "Council forces approaching! We have minutes, maybe less!"

Aria's heart raced, but she kept her voice calm as she delivered her final message.

"Remember, you are not alone in this. We are all awakening together. Feel, live, love - be human. This is Aria Thorne, and we are the dawn of a new..."

The feed cut off as the first explosions rocked the building. Evan was at her side in an instant, pulling her toward the exit.

"Go!" David yelled over the chaos. "We'll hold them off!"

Aria wanted to argue, to stay and fight. But she knew their mission was bigger than any one moment, any one place.

As they fled into the night, the city around them pulsated with newfound life. Aria could feel it in the air - fear, yes, but also hope, joy, a thousand other emotions too complex to name.

They had done it. They had awakened a city from its emotional slumber. And though the fight was far from over, in that moment, racing through streets alive with emotion, Aria knew they had already won the most important battle.

The world was awakening. And nothing would ever be the same.

TWENTY-THREE

THE EYE OF THE STORM

Aria's lungs burned as she and Evan raced through the chaotic streets. The sounds of the chase faded behind them, replaced by a cacophony of emotional voices. Laughter, screams, cries of joy and anger - the city was alive in a way she'd never experienced before.

They ducked into an alley and pressed against the cool brick wall. Evan's breath came in ragged gasps beside her. "Do you think we lost them?"

Aria nodded, her own chest heaving. "For now. But they won't stop looking."

As her heartbeat slowed, the reality of their situation settled over her like a heavy blanket. They were cut off from their team, their safe house compromised. And the city... the city was teetering on the brink of either revolution or total collapse.

"We need to regroup," Evan said, voicing her thoughts. "Find the others, come up with a new plan."

Aria closed her eyes and forced herself to think. Where

would the team go if they got separated? What had been their contingency?

Her eyes snapped open. "The old library. In Sector 9. It was our emergency rendezvous point."

Evan nodded, a small smile tugging at his lips despite the gravity of their situation. "Good memory. Let's go."

They moved cautiously through the streets, marveling at the transformation around them. People embraced openly, their faces alive with a myriad of expressions. But there was also fear and confusion. More than once, they had to bypass crowds of citizens overwhelmed by their newfound emotions.

"We did this," Aria murmured, a mixture of pride and guilt churning in her stomach. "All this joy, all this pain... it's because of us."

Evan's hand found hers and squeezed gently. "We gave them their humanity back, Aria. Whatever happens now, that's worth fighting for."

As they approached Sector 9, the crowds thinned. This area had always been quieter, home to the city's dwindling intellectual class. The old library stood like a sentinel, its weathered stone facade a stark contrast to the sleek modernity around it.

They slipped inside, the musty smell of old books enveloping them. For a moment, the chaos outside seemed distant, muffled.

"Aria? Evan?" A familiar voice called from the shadows.

Relief washed over Aria as Zara emerged from behind a pile of books, followed closely by Tom and David. They looked battered and exhausted, but alive.

"Thank God," David said, his usually stoic face betraying real emotion. "We feared the worst when we were separated."

Quick hugs were exchanged, the physical contact a reminder of how far they'd all come from their emotionally repressed past.

"Maya?" Aria asked, noticing the absence of her newest ally.

Tom's face fell. "We... we're not sure. She provided cover for our escape, and then..."

The unfinished sentence hung in the air, heavy with implication.

Aria swallowed hard, pushing down the guilt and worry. They couldn't afford to dwell on maybes right now. "Okay. What's our status? What are we working with?"

Zara pulled out a battered tablet, her fingers flying over the cracked screen. "It's a mixed bag. The good news is that the Awakening is spreading faster than we ever imagined. Nearly 70% of the city's population is showing signs of emotional awakening."

"And the bad news?" Evan asked.

David's face was grim. "The Council is gearing up for a final push. They're rallying their remaining loyal Enforcers for what looks like a last-ditch effort to regain control."

Aria's mind raced, weighing options, calculating risks. "We need to counter them. Make a last stand of our own."

"How?" Tom asked, his voice tinged with both excitement and fear. "We're outnumbered, outgunned."

A plan began to form in Aria's mind, bold and dangerous, but potentially game-changing. "We use their own weapon against them. The emotion suppression network-we turn it into an awakening catalyst."

The others stared at her, a mixture of awe and skepticism on their faces.

"Is that even possible?" David asked.

Zara's eyes brightened with understanding. "Theoretically, yes. The neural net was designed to dampen emotional signals in the brain. If we could reverse the polarity and amplify those signals instead..."

"We could wake up the entire city at once," Evan finished, excitement building in his voice.

Aria nodded, feeling a wave of hope. "Exactly. But to do that, we'd need access to the central control hub. At the heart of the Emotional Regulation Center."

A heavy silence fell over the group as the enormity of the task sank in.

"It's suicide," Tom said quietly. "The Center will be the most heavily guarded place in the city."

"Probably," Aria agreed. "But it's also our best chance to end this once and for all."

She looked around at her team - her family. They were tired, scared, pushed to their limits. But in their eyes, she saw the same determination that burned within her.

"I'm not going to lie," she said, her voice steady. "This will be dangerous. Perhaps impossible. I'm not asking any of you to come with me. But I must try."

Evan stepped forward without hesitation. "I'm with you. Always."

One by one, the others nodded in agreement.

"Well," Zara said with a wry smile, "I always wanted to go out in a blaze of glory. Might as well make it count."

Aria felt a lump form in her throat, overwhelmed by the loyalty and courage of her friends. "Thank you," she managed. "To all of you."

As they began to plan their attack on the Emotional Regulation Center, Aria felt a strange calm settle over her. Whatever happened next, they would face it together. And win or lose, they would do it with the full depth of their reclaimed humanity.

The final battle for the emotional freedom of the city was about to begin. And Aria was ready to lead the charge.

TWENTY-FOUR

THE HEART OF FEELING

The Emotional Regulation Center loomed before them, a monolith of steel and glass that seemed to absorb the light around it. Aria's heart pounded in her chest, a mixture of fear and determination coursing through her veins.

"Everyone clear on the plan?" she asked, her voice barely above a whisper.

Nods all around. They had spent hours preparing, going over every detail, every contingency. Now it was time to put it all into action.

Zara's fingers danced over her tablet one last time. "Okay, I've looped in the external security feeds. We have a five minute window before they notice the discrepancy."

"Then let's not waste it," Evan said, his hand finding Aria's and squeezing it gently.

They moved quickly, using the cover of the early morning darkness. The city around them was eerily quiet, as if holding its breath in anticipation of what was to come.

At the service entrance, David made quick work of the lock. Years of maintaining the Center's systems had given him an intimate knowledge of its weaknesses.

Inside, the sterile corridors seemed to go on forever. Aria felt a shiver run down her spine as memories of her time as a Collector threatened to overwhelm her. But she pushed them aside and focused on the task at hand.

Three levels down, they encountered their first real resistance. A pair of Enforcers rounded the corner, their eyes widening in recognition.

"Halt!" one shouted, reaching for his weapon.

But Tom was quicker. The vial of Emotional Catalyst he threw shattered at their feet, releasing a cloud of shimmering particles. The Enforcers stumbled, gasping as the full weight of long-suppressed emotions hit them.

"I'm sorry," Tom said quietly as they hurried past the disoriented men. "And thank you."

Aria felt a pang in her chest. Even now, even after everything, it hurt to see the pain of the awakening. But it was necessary. It was right.

They pressed on, deeper into the heart of the center. With each level they descended, the security grew tighter, the challenges more daunting. But they had surprise on their side, and the desperate courage of those who fought for something they believed in with every fiber of their being.

Finally, they reached the central control center. The massive door loomed before them, its surface a maze of locks and security measures.

"This is it," Zara said, her voice taut with tension. "Once we're inside, we'll have maybe ten minutes before the full force of the Council's security comes down on us."

Aria nodded and took a deep breath. "Then we'd better make those ten minutes count."

It took all of Zara's hacking skills and David's technical knowledge to breach the door. When it finally slid open with a pneumatic hiss, they rushed inside, ready for anything.

Except for what they found.

The control center was a cavernous room filled with banks of humming computers and holographic displays. And in the center, standing in front of the main console, was a familiar figure.

"Mom?" Aria gasped, barely daring to believe her eyes.

Dr. Elena Thorne turned, her face a mask of conflicting emotions. "Aria. I've been waiting for you."

For a moment, no one moved. The air crackled with tension and unspoken questions.

Then Evan's voice, deep and urgent: "Aria, we don't have much time."

It broke the spell. Aria stepped forward, her mind spinning. "Mom, what are you... how are you here?"

Dr. Thorne's lips curved into a sad smile. "Did you think I wouldn't notice my own daughter dismantling my life's work? I've been watching you, Aria. All of you. And I knew you'd come here eventually."

"To stop you," Aria said, her voice stronger now. "To undo what you've done to the city, to all those people."

"No," Dr. Thorne shook his head. "To finish what I started."

Confusion swept through the group. Aria felt like the

ground was shifting beneath her feet. "What do you mean?"

Dr. Thorne turned back to the console, her fingers flying over the controls. "The Emotional Regulation Initiative was never meant to be permanent. It was a stopgap, a way to give humanity a chance to reset, to learn to manage their emotions in a healthier way."

Images flashed across the screens around them-data, formulas, plans that spanned decades.

"But the Council," Dr. Thorne continued, her voice tight with old anger, "they saw the power in keeping people suppressed indefinitely. They twisted my work, perverted its purpose."

Aria's mind reeled as the pieces fell into place. "The fail-safes. The potential for awakening. They built them into the system from the beginning."

Her mother nodded, a gleam of pride in her eyes. "I always hoped someone would figure it out. I just never imagined it would be my own daughter."

The moment was shattered by the sound of the alarm. Zara's voice, tight with panic: "We've got incoming! Lots of incoming!"

Aria made a split-second decision. "Mom, we're here to reverse the suppression field, to wake up the whole city at once. Will you help us?"

Dr. Thorne hesitated only a moment before nodding. "It is time. It's time."

What followed was a frantic race against the clock. Aria and her mother worked in tandem, their hands flying over the controls while the others provided support and defense.

The sound of the approaching Enforcers grew louder with each passing second.

"Almost there," Dr. Thorne murmured, her face tight with concentration. "Just one more..."

The door exploded inward in a shower of sparks and twisted metal. Enforcers poured through the opening, weapons raised.

"Step away from the console!" a familiar voice commanded. Director Kaine strode in, his face a mask of cold fury.

Aria moved to stand between the Enforcers and her mother, her heart pounding but her voice steady. "It's over, Director. We're waking everyone. All of them. You can't stop it."

Kaine's eyes blazed with a mixture of anger and... was that fear? "You have no idea what you're doing. The chaos, the pain you'll unleash."

"No," Aria countered, feeling the strength of her convictions, her reclaimed emotions, filling her. "We're giving people back their humanity. Their choice. It may be messy, it may be hard, but it's real. It's alive."

For a moment, there was a tense silence in the room, two ideologies on the brink of collision.

Then, with a soft chime, Dr. Thorne's voice said, "It's done.

A wave of energy pulsed outward from the center of the room. Aria felt it wash over her, warm and alive and indescribably powerful. Around her, she saw the Enforcers stumble, their faces contorting as long-buried emotions surfaced.

Kaine fell to his knees, a cry of fear and wonder torn from his throat.

And beyond the walls of the center, Aria could almost feel the city awakening. Millions of minds and hearts suddenly alive with the full spectrum of human emotion.

As the wave subsided, Aria turned to her friends - her family. Their faces lit up with tears and laughter, the joy of victory mixed with the weight of all they'd been through.

"We did it," she breathed, barely able to believe it. "We really did it."

Evan pulled her into a fierce hug, his voice thick with emotion. "You did it, Aria. You woke up the world."

As they held each other, surrounded by the sounds of a city relearning how to feel, Aria knew the real work was just beginning. There would be challenges ahead, pain and confusion as people grappled with their newfound emotions.

But as she looked at the faces around her - her mother, her friends, even the awakening Enforcers - she felt a surge of hope. They had given humanity its heart back. And together, they would learn to use it wisely.

The dawn of a new, sentient world had come. And Aria was ready to face it with every emotion she'd fought so hard to reclaim.

EPILOGUE: A WORLD REBORN

Aria stood at the window of her office and watched the sunset paint the city in shades of gold and pink. Even after six months, the sight still took her breath away. Had the world always been this vibrant, this alive?

A knock at the door brought her out of her reverie. "Come in," she called, turning to see Evan enter, a warm smile on his face.

"I thought I'd find you here," he said, crossing the room to stand beside her. His hand found hers, their fingers intertwining in a gesture that had become as natural as breathing. "Big day tomorrow. How are you feeling?"

Aria let out a breath, a mix of emotions swirling inside her. "Nervous. Excited. Terrified. Take your pick."

Evan chuckled, the sound sending a pleasant shiver down her spine. "So, the usual, then?"

She nudged his arm playfully, but couldn't help the smile that tugged at her lips. "This isn't just another day, Evan. Tomorrow we begin to phase out the last of the emotional stabilizers. People will be completely on their own with their feelings for the first time since... well, ever."

Evan's expression sobered, but his eyes remained warm. "I know. But, Aria, look how far we've come. The city is thriving. People are learning, growing, feeling. We've got this."

Aria nodded, letting his confidence bolster her own. She turned back to the window and took in the city stretching out before them. The changes were everywhere, if you knew where to look. Art galleries had sprung up in once-abandoned buildings. Music drifted out of open windows. And everywhere, people moved with a new energy, their faces alive with expressions that would have been unthinkable just a few months ago.

"You're right," she said quietly. "It's just... sometimes I can hardly believe we did it. That this is real."

A commotion in the hallway interrupted their moment. The door burst open, revealing a breathless Zara. "Guys! You need to see this!"

They followed her into the main operations room, where screens displayed feeds from all over the city. Tom and David were already there, their faces a mixture of concern and excitement.

"What's going on?" Aria asked, slipping into command mode.

David gestured to the center screen. "It's the old Council building. People have gathered there, hundreds of them."

Aria's heart raced as she took in the scene. A crowd had indeed gathered outside the imposing structure that had once housed the city's unemotional leadership. But this was no riot or protest. As she watched, people began to sing, their voices rising in a melody that sent shivers down her spine.

"Is that..." Evan began, his voice full of wonder.

"The ancient anthem of the city," Tom finished, his eyes shining with unshed tears. "I found references to it in the archives, but I never thought..."

Aria felt a lump form in her throat as the chant swelled. It wasn't perfect - the voices cracked with emotion, some missed notes altogether. But it was real, raw, and beautiful in a way that defied description.

"They remembered," she whispered, awe in her voice. "All along, deep down, they remembered."

As they watched, more people joined the crowd. Strangers hugged, laughed, cried together. It was messy and chaotic and absolutely stunning.

"I think," Zara said, a rare softness in her voice, "this is what hope looks like."

Aria felt Evan's arm slip around her waist, anchoring her as emotions threatened to overwhelm her. She leaned into him, drawing strength from his presence.

"We should go down there," Tom suggested, already halfway to the door. "Be with them."

Aria hesitated for a moment, old instincts fighting with new feelings. But as she looked at the faces of her friends - her family - she knew there was only one choice.

"You're right," she said, straightening her shoulders. "Let's go."

As they made their way through the streets, Aria marveled at how much had changed. The rigid order of the old world had given way to something more organic, more alive. It wasn't perfect - there were still struggles, still pain. But it was real.

They reached the edge of the crowd just as the song ended. For a moment there was silence. Then, as if by unspoken agreement, people began to share stories. Of their first memories of feeling. Of the joy and pain of rediscovering love, grief, anger, hope.

An older woman approached Aria, her eyes filled with tears. "You're her, aren't you? The one who woke us?"

Aria felt a blush creep across her cheeks. "I... we all did. It was a team effort."

The woman reached out and took Aria's hand in both of hers. "Thank you," she said, her voice thick with emotion. "For giving us our hearts back."

As more people noticed her, a ripple went through the crowd. But there was no anger, no resentment for the turmoil they had caused. Instead, Aria saw gratitude, respect, and a fierce determination to make the most of this second chance at a full life.

Someone began to sing again, and soon the entire gathering had joined in. This time, Aria let her own voice rise with theirs, feeling the vibrations in her chest, the connection to each person around her.

As the sun dipped below the horizon, painting the sky in a riot of color, Aria looked at the faces around her. Evan, his eyes bright with love and pride. Zara, her usual cynicism tempered by genuine joy. Tom and David, who had risked everything for this moment.

And beyond them, a town full of people learning to live and love wholeheartedly. There would be challenges ahead, she knew. The road to true emotional health was long and often difficult. But looking at the hope and determination that shone in every face, Aria knew they would face it together.

They had reclaimed their humanity, their ability to feel the full range of emotions. And in doing so, they had given birth to a world more beautiful and complex than they had ever imagined.

As the stars began to appear in the darkening sky, Aria felt a deep sense of peace settle over her. Whatever came next, they were ready. Ready to feel, to love, to live - fully human at last.

The emotion collector had done her job. And a new chapter was about to begin.

The End